About the Author

JENNIFER WALLACE grew up in London and Edinburgh and studied Classics and English at Cambridge University. She now teaches English Literature there, specialising in the Romantic poets and in tragic drama. Research for some of her previous books – on Romantic Hellenism and on the archaeological imagination – has led her to follow Byron's footsteps through the Pindus mountains on the Albanian/Greek border and to swim into a cave in the Belize jungle, in search of the Mayan entrance to the underworld. She has worked as a freelance journalist for British and American publications on stories ranging from Israel-Palestine to tribal India. She has also played double bass in a jazz quartet. *Digging Up Milton* is Jennifer's

D1350699

www.JenniferWallace.

04325333

DIGGING UP MILTON

JENNIFER WALLACE

Cillian Press |

First published in Great Britain in 2015
by Cillian Press Limited. 83 Ducie Street, Manchester M1 2JQ
www.cillianpress.co.uk

British Library Cataloguing in Publication Data.
A catalogue record for this book is available from the British Library.

Paperback ISBN: 978-1-909776-10-4
eBook ISBN: 978-1-909776-11-1

Soil Photo © Zlatko Antic - Dreamstime.com
Author Photograph © Robert Wallis

Published by Cillian Press
Manchester - United Kingdom - 2015
www.cillianpress.co.uk

To my father, Fleming Wallace

Historical Note

Philip Neve really published a short, 34-page pamphlet, entitled *A Narrative of the Disinterment of Milton's Coffin, in the Parish-Church of St Giles, Cripplegate*, in 1790. I have included an extract from this pamphlet in chapter 8 and another extract from the second edition, published two months later, in chapter 12.

The two reports from *The Public Advertiser*, in chapters 6 and 9, are also taken *verbatim* from the original newspaper.

Quotations from John Milton are taken from *Paradise Lost*, edited by John Leonard (London: Penguin Classics, 2000) and *John Milton: The Major Works*, edited by Stephen Orgel and Jonathan Goldberg (Oxford: Oxford World's Classics, 2003).

Everything else, including the postscripts, is the work of fiction.

A plaque, recording the place of John Milton's burial, can still be seen on the floor at the front of the nave in St Giles' Church, Cripplegate, which is nowadays surrounded by the modern Barbican in London.

The ultimate fate of Milton's bones has never been conclusively determined.

Of man's first disobedience, and the fruit
Of that forbidden tree, whose mortal taste
Brought death into the world, and all our woe,
With loss of Eden, till one greater man
Restore us, and regain the blissful seat,
Sing Heav'nly Muse...

                ... what in me is dark
Illumine, what is low raise and support;
That to the height of this great argument
I may assert Eternal Providence,
And justify the ways of God to men

(Paradise Lost Book 1)

BOOK 1

It was on the night of 3rd August in the year of our Lord 1790 that I first learned from my husband of the fateful unearthing of Mr Milton's coffin, an event that was to change my life forever.

Little, of course, did I think then, on that hot summer night, that the business – exciting though it was – would come to play such an important part in my subsequent fortunes. Scarcely did I reflect then that I would be undone on account of a few old bones, when all around me were joyous and puffed up by the news of their discovery.

The first I knew that the poet had been raised was when my husband, Mr Nathaniel Grant, returned late from a merry-meeting at Fountain's tavern, reeling and staggering along Beech Street like an old cart with one loose wheel. I could not remember the last time I had witnessed him so intoxicated – he is apt to be a very steady, sober man, of which more anon – and I was not a little alarmed and amused in equal measure. But I assisted him to our chair, and he pulled me down to sit upon his lap.

'Come here, Lizzie my love,' says he. 'I've been drinking, as you can see.'

'No, Mr Grant,' I quipped, 'you are surely mistaken, for I never saw a more sober man.' (I like to tease him so.)

'I've been drinking,' continued he, 'with the men and, with every flask of ale we have emptied, another toast was raised. "*Long live King George!*" cried Mr Tucker, a patriot if ever there was one, and "*Long live Tom Paine!*" shouted young Benjamin Holmes, the hot-headed journeyman, in reply. Well, at that point, Mrs G, the house descended into such a tumult of cries and laughter and passion that I truly believed the very Frenchies were among us and stirring us all to revolution.'

I laughed at that point because Mr Grant thinks of very little else besides the revolution in France and is always worrying the Frenchies will be coming over to our country and mingling with our society and turning us all into radicals.

'But then Mr Cole (the church-warden no less) grabbed a new cup of ale,' said my husband, 'and he leapt upon the table. We were overcome with surprise and fell suddenly silent. "*Long live John Milton*" – declared he – "*that was raised again today*".'

'Lord! Mr Grant' – cried I – 'is not that the great Bard?'

'Indeed it is the very same,' said he. 'The man who penned the most sublime epic since antiquity and dared to *justify the ways of God to men.*' (Mr Grant had more education than almost any man in Cripplegate and has read the Bard's great epic.)

'So husband,' asked I, 'how was he discovered?'

'It was seven days ago now,' said he, 'that Mr Cole ordered the workmen to dig in search of the coffin.'

'I thought something was amiss' – interjected I – 'for the church has been closed an age and very little progress to show for it.'

'For many a year,' continued he, ignoring me as usual, 'for many a year, as you know well, Mrs G, the tradition has been that Milton was buried in the church, but the exact location has been uncertain. We thought it was in the chancel, under the clerk's desk. Indeed we show enquirers the spot under the clerk's desk, in the present chancel, as the place of Milton's interment, but it may well have been in a different position entirely. After all, the church has been altered since Milton's day. I believe, after some inquiry into the matter, that the position of the chancel was moved some hundred years ago and thus the poet may be presumed to lie in a different place entirely.'

'Yes, yes!' cried I crossly, for Mr Grant is apt to be most tedious on these points. 'But it is of no matter, for men will believe what they wish. Nay, it was only last year, husband, that I shewed a visitor the place below the clerk's desk, and he was most moved by the sight and thanked me warmly for my pains with a gift of threepence!'

'Men can be most foolish sometimes,' replied he, 'but we demand to know the truth. So while the church is under general repair, Mr Strong and Mr Cole have prudently judged that a search can be made without too much inconvenience, and to this end they requested the workmen to dig, without of course telling them the illustrious object of their search, lest there be any foul play.'

'Wise, indeed,' said I. 'There is no telling what men might do if they know the value of their quest.'

'Indeed, Lizzie. I said as much to Mr Cole. Some things are best kept to ourselves,' said he. 'Anyway, several days have passed and the workmen have found no joy, although they were working fit to waken the dead, breaking the stone floor and burrowing under the common-council-men's pew.'

'That's tough' – quipped I – 'for all the councillors' weight over the years must have packed that ground down hard.'

'Hush, Mrs G' – said he – 'you speak most unfairly! This afternoon came word from the church – a coffin had been discovered! We all three hastened immediately to the church, I having at that time only two more letters to copy for Mr Strong in the day, and a certain excitement growing strong within our breasts. Mr Cole had thought to bring a candle with him, which shewed much foresight, for when we arrived at the church we found that the burial place in question was right under the common-council-men's pew, and we could have discerned nothing without its aid.'

'What did you see? Was it the poet?' (Mr Grant was telling the story

11

too slowly for my liking, and I was growing impatient.)

'Stepping down into the pit, which had been opened beneath the pew, I could see one leaden coffin, much corroded, and directly below it, a second, wooden, coffin. According to Mr Strong, the wooden coffin was that of Milton's father. "John Milton, Nathaniel", he declared to me excitedly, "was always reported to be buried next to his father, and here we see" – and he pointed – "one coffin does indeed lie beside the other". Our hearts were all beating wildly by this time and I was thinking, wife, that this discovery could mean a change in all our fortunes.'

And he blushed a little for shame as he said this. But I clasped his hand with delight.

'Indeed it might, Mr G, and not before time neither! For you surely deserve some good fortune.' (He has been suffering from the most miserable state of affairs, but of this I will speak more later.)

'Mr Cole and Mr Strong examined the leaden coffin,' said my husband, 'and then they ordered me to fetch water and a brush that they might wash it, in search of an inscription, or initials, or date – I went to the shoemaker on the corner, and demanded these things of his boy, and he quickly brought them to the church – But even after Mr Cole and I had carefully cleaned the coffin and brushed down all its contours, nothing was to be seen. There was no inscription!'

'O, disappointment indeed, Mr G,' quoth I. 'Can we be sure the coffin is that of Mr Milton?'

'It seems most probable that it is' – says my husband – 'there being no other coffins found in the vicinity, from the present chancel to the pillar, and besides the second wooden coffin beneath seems to point to this identification. Indeed I was even so bold as to suggest to Mr Strong that we raise the coffin to examine the one below, there being a greater chance, in my opinion, of finding some inscription upon the latter. But Mr Strong seemed certain that we had found the coffin of John Milton, and not wishing to disturb the sacred ashes that such a removal could entail, he resisted my proposal. So Mr Cole ordered the ground to be closed, and Mr Strong seemed satisfied and departed to his house in Red Cross Street.'

'This seems to be a long story about very little,' cried I, 'a tale only of a leaden box which could have contained the bones of any man! Why do you excite me in this way, and all for a dusty casket, which may be empty for all we know? And here was I thinking that this would mean gold and riches and some mighty change in our fortunes.'

'Peace, woman,' he said, 'for I have only just begun the story.'

I confess that I have never seen my husband so filled with quiet excitement and eager hope as he was that night. He is not the most effusive of gentlemen, but that evening his eyes sparkled and his gestures were animated and he cared not that his wig was a little askew. His voice had grown stronger and less slurred with drink during the narration, and he sat forward on the edge of his chair, hardly able to keep still. By then I had drawn up a little stool at his feet and held his hand, looking up at his shining face as the taper burned low beside us.

'Mr Strong having left us,' continued he, 'Mr Cole took hold of my arm and suggested that we retire to Mr Fountain's house in Beech Street close by, to celebrate our discovery, as he put it, and drink a toast to the poet's soul. So we caroused there for the evening, Mrs G—'

'So I can tell, husband' – I interjected – 'it must be ten ales that you have tippled, if you have had one!'

'It was a merry evening, indeed,' he replied, 'and old Mr Laming the pawnbroker was there too, and a Mr Taylor, a surgeon, visiting from Derbyshire, with many a tale to tell of affairs in the North Countrys – but Mr Cole would keep boasting that we had raised the shade of Milton, until this moment, which I told you of, when he shouted a toast to the Bard before the whole house, and that truly set everyone a-talking and questioning us about the doings of the afternoon. I was feeling that this was a matter we should keep to ourselves, Lizzie, especially given Mr Strong's evident delicate sensitivity about the matter, but Mr Cole was full of the story, and telling everyone about the two coffins, the lead and the wood, and the lack of inscriptions, and – as he put it – the terrible *mystery* of the tale.'

Mr Cole does indeed often speak more than he should. I think he likes to draw attention to himself, since he is a vain man and proud of his elevation to the position of church-warden. Time was – I can remember – when he was no more than Johnny Cole, the message boy, running up and down Beech Street with errands for the vicar and the folk in the big Drewry House. But he has a talent for making men notice him, with his jet black hair (still his own) and his flashing eyes and his sense of drama, and that, together with his supposed ease of temper, ensured that he was promoted, two years ago, to church-warden. I did not think, at the time, that he was suited to the ordinary tasks of keeping the church safe, but he seemed so high in everyone's estimation, especially that of Mr Strong and even Mr Grant, that I kept my mouth shut.

My husband was continuing with his tale. After all the commotion in the tavern, and Mr Cole's dramatic story, finally Mr Laming, the pawnbroker, had spoken out. 'Might we not see the coffin?' And at once, my husband said, the crowd had joined in. 'Yes, we must see this coffin, for he is the most famous poet of our land.' 'And the most honest and patriotic Englishman,' Mr Tucker had added, from the corner table, his eyes shining and round as pewter plates. As their shouts arose, Mr Cole had assented, agreeing that if the ground be not already closed, the closing of it should be deferred until they had satisfied their curiosity.

'And so the conclusion, wife,' said Mr Grant, 'is that tomorrow morning, early, between 7 and 8 o'clock, we shall go to the church with Mr Laming and Mr Fountain, and examine the coffin again, before it is re-interred.'

'What excitement!' quoth I. 'A holy resurrection in our church! May I come to witness this deed?'

'I am not certain that the tender sex may be present,' he replied. 'We do not know the nature of the casket. It looks so old it may fall apart at any time, and who knows whether the contents are fit for gentle viewing.'

'Larks, sir!' cried I. 'I have seen plenty in my time! There's many an occasion, when I have been digging a grave for Mrs Hoppey, that my spade has gone clean through a rotting casket and spilled the stinking remains into the hole. Besides,' said I, 'you need somebody to help with cleaning and to watch out for Mr Strong.'

'You're a plucky woman, Lizzie,' he said, putting an arm around me as he rose to his unsteady feet and giving me a squeeze. 'I'm a lucky man, to be sure,' and he staggered back upon the bed and fell immediately into a loud snore, which travelled the length of Beech Street and must surely have troubled Milton in his eternal sleep.

*

The following morning I was up bright and early before the sunrise, washing and cleaning and fetching the water, so as to have all the tasks done before the great deed of the day. When Mr Grant arose from his bed and I placed his morning's porridge before him, I had already put two hours' work behind me. We left the house sometime before 7, armed with some brushes, cloths, a candle and a knife, just in case something needed to be prised open, as my husband said. Mr Fountain met us at the next corner, and Mr Taylor, who was staying at Fountain's, appeared too, yawning and rubbing his eyes like pudding pastry, and we picked up old Mr Laming at his house down Red Cross Street, and then we all walked along to Mr Ascough's, the coffin-maker, to ask for Holmes, his apprentice, since he had been so forward the night before with his knowledge of caskets and boxes and diverse burials of many kinds. He came to the door rapidly, coughing and bearing a large spade and a rope upon his shoulder, and we all proceeded to the church, I a little retiring on account of being the only woman present, and hanging onto my husband's arm for support.

Once inside the church, my husband led the group to the pit below the common-council-men's pew, and showed them the coffin, lying deep in the ground. I stayed standing beside the pew, not venturing down into the pit, but I could not prevent myself from peering below the wooden floor of the pew to see the box which supposedly contained the bones of the man whose poetry I have never read – in faith, I confess I can scarcely read at all! – but of whose life and importance I have heard many men tell in recent times. I can hardly describe my feelings those first few minutes. My heart was trembling with awe and trepidation and reverence, just as it was the first time that I met Mr Grant, but I'll tell you more of that fateful meeting later. How blessed am I, I thought, to be standing so close to the last resting place of the man whom my husband says was the truest son England ever had! And how unfortunate is it – I continued – that I cannot read a word he wrote and that he is dead and cannot speak his stern and manly verses for my delight. And I bemoaned my state, that I must forever be on the outside, shut off from the world of words, which makes my husband red with fiery passion.

The men had now, with some difficulty, pulled the leaden coffin up out of the pit and into the daylight on the stone, flagged floor. I could see it better now, black and dusty, with one corroded hole open large enough for vermin to scurry through at the coffin's foot. We all stood silent for a few minutes, staring down at the box. I have thought since that, had we but realised, we had the chance then to leave the dead in peace and continue to live a blessed life, but at the time we thought only that we were standing as if upon the brink of a vast and thrilling chasm, which we could choose to enter or ignore.

'What say you, that we take a quick peek at the man?' whispers old Mr Laming after a while, crouching down beside the box and holding his lighted candle to the hole. I could see his thin, eager nose was already picking up some noxious scent from the cavity, but try as he might, he could not cast his candle's light far into the black hollow.

'It's enough surely that we have studied his coffin,' replies my husband. 'Mr Strong was most forceful yesterday that it should not be disturbed.'

'Good God, Grant, have some courage, sir!' cries Mr Fountain. 'We have not come this close to regarding the remains of our greatest poet, only to re-bury them without reward. What harm can it do, just to prize open the lid a little? It is but a small thing to nail it closed again.'

My husband shook his head uncertainly, and it seemed as if he and Mr Fountain might continue to argue for some time, but Mr Laming and Mr Taylor now regained their former energy, and also urged Holmes to open the coffin, that they might see the body. Holmes was happy to oblige, for he was as seized by the unholy desire to view the body of the Bard as the rest of us (my husband, were he to admit it, included), and so he ran back to his house to fetch a mallet and a chisel, which he had neglected to bring, and was in no time at all returned with the tools. He proceeded to cut open the top of the coffin, and then peel back the leaden sheet slowly.

We all gasped. The body appeared perfect! I could see the outline of a head, wrapped in a shroud, the shoulders well defined, the chest proud and sturdy, the ribs standing up regularly! The body was about five feet five inches in length, about the same fine length and shape as Mr Grant when he lies in our bed beside me. But the whole was wrapped in a winding sheet, so that we could discern only the contours of the body and not the visage or the characteristicks.

'Let's see the rascal!' said Mr Laming, trying to lighten the mood with a quip, and when the others nodded assent vigorously around him, he steps forward with alacrity and pulls back the shroud. Immediately the chest collapsed on account, Mr Taylor explained, of the ribs crumbling inside. No matter, the face and head were still perfect!

''Tis no doubt 'tis Milton,' whispers my husband at last, while everyone was silent with astonishment. 'The poet may have been blind but he had a fine head of hair by all accounts, and – look – this man's hair is still luxurious and fair.' He touched one of the yellow-brown strands and it came away in his hands, like a well-boiled leek that's tender and ripe for eating.

'Let me touch the sacred body,' says Mr Fountain, not wanting to be outdone by my husband. For there has long been a rivalry between them, on account of me and my past history, but of that I will tell you more later. 'Let me touch the sacred body,' says Mr Fountain, and he runs his hand all over the face, feeling in the eye sockets, which were empty and corrupt, and over the fine, bony nose and even inside the mouth. In the mouth his fingers stopped – for I was watching most particularly – and he seemed to hold onto one of the teeth. He was quietly pulling it and pulling it, but it would not come, and the others were now examining the chest and not paying attention, and my husband was lost in his own meditations and oblivious to what was taking place. But I saw Mr Fountain's difficulty, and so I bent down and picked up a stone off the floor – for the floor was all broken up and pitted on account of the workmen and the repair – and I steps forward and – 'I'll help you, Mr F,' I says in a low voice and brought that stone down hard on the side of the face, and all the teeth and the upper and lower jaw fell out in Mr Fountain's hand. Mr Laming and Mr Taylor both looked up, and I stood proud and beaming at my efforts, and Mr Fountain held out the treasure for everyone to see. There were but five teeth in the upper jaw, all gleaming white and sound, and four in the lower jaw. Mr Laming took three teeth and Mr Taylor took two.

'What will you give me,' I whispers, 'who knocked this treasure out for you. And not the first treasure I've given you in my life, neither.' And I winked – of which more later – and held out my hand, and he gave me the upper-jaw with two white teeth still in it.

'You are still a great gal, Lizzie,' he murmured and shot a glance at

Mr Grant, but he was standing a little way off still staring at the lock of hair in his hand in stupefaction and not aware of anything we did.

I slipped the jaw into my bosom, and says – 'This is our secret, Mr Fountain. Never breathe a word to any man!' And all morning, when I felt the awkward corners of the jaw press painfully upon my chest, I thought with pleasure of Mr Fountain and the private transaction between us.

Mr Laming now was working on the whole head. I saw him look at the lower jaw bone which Mr Fountain had left on the side of the council-men's pew, while he was whispering with me, and pick it up as if to put it in his pocket with the other teeth. But then he must have thought that the hair had more value than the jaw or something (I could see his mind revolving quickly over what Mr Grant had told us and making its calculations, something he is accustomed to doing in his pawnbroking business), because he tossed the bone back into the coffin and fell upon the locks of hair with serious purpose. He raised the head, which was damp and mobile between his hands like clay upon a potter's wheel, and I could see the hair beneath, thick and straight, combed and tied together for interment, and the stench caught the back of my throat, worse than the stink of the dung wharf at Blackfriars when the summer heat hangs heavy upon it.

'I see we need a cutting machine, Fountain,' says old Laming, and drops the head again back into the noxious sludge. Mr Fountain, Mr Taylor and Holmes left with him, to fetch scissors to cut off some hair, and Mr Grant and I were left alone with the body.

'A wonderful day, Mr Grant! How exciting a discovery!' I ventured. But he sat on the pew, still staring at that lock of hair, and shaking his head sorrowfully.

'I fear it is a foul thing we have done, wife,' he said. 'We have broken open the body of a saint and God knows what terrible punishments, what *perpetual banishment* indeed, may follow.'

'Nonsense!' I cried, impatient as always with my husband's caution.

Sometimes he is apt to seem too old and narrow in his ways, more than the 20 years that lie between us. 'Nobody will be banished anywhere and God will know nothing about it! And besides,' I added, pleased with myself for this new argument had just occurred to me, 'if this is a saint, then we have but taken holy reliques.'

Mr Grant had no reply to this since he held the relique of the hair in his very hand, and had not only failed to stop the other men but had even been the first to touch the body and thus show how easily parts could be removed. So we sat and waited for the other men in silence, each musing on very different thoughts.

Soon the men returned and set about the head again, poking at it with a stick to avoid getting the evil-smelling sludge upon their hands. Mr Taylor reached in with his scissors but as he touched the hair, which now had been pulled up over the forehead, he found it came away in a thick bunch in his hand. Mr Laming and Mr Fountain also reached in and grabbed a big handful of hair, thick as a clump of a fodder for the stable-horse, and then even my husband, who had been sitting weakly at the side but was anxious perhaps that the hair would all be seized by men who could not understand its value, pushed into the group and, with a cry of, 'For God's sake men, shew some respect!' he took the scissors from Mr Laming and carefully snipped the final locks from over the brow. I was proud of him at that moment, and my heart swelled to think that I had so noble and well-educated a husband. And Mr Laming, who by this time had got hold of one of the leg bones and was waving it about, no doubt calculating the cost of each piece once they would be cut up in slices, was stopped in his tracks and made to abandon his plans for the shanks, dropping the bones back into the coffin dejectedly.

The mood of the men was changing, maybe as a result of my husband's words. After the frenzy and excitement of the dissection, which had been as heated and tumultuous as any bull baiting, that's for certain, a weary silence descended.

'Let us amend what we can,' said my husband, 'for who knows what Mr Strong or even Mr Cole will think of our actions.' And he bent back the lid of the coffin, where it had been peeled away to reveal the head and the foot, so that it now half concealed the plunder beneath, and the other men helped him drag the casket back from the edge of the excavation and down to its original station beneath the pew.

'What shall we do now?' says young Holmes anxiously. 'The workmen will be here presently and the coffin should not be left unattended. My master, Mr Ascough, is from home, and Mrs Hoppey, the sexton, is also from home the whole day, and I must finish the making of two coffins by the evening.'

'My wife can keep watch,' says my husband, smiling at me. 'She is not afeard to stand in the church alone, and besides, she has watched me sleeping many a night.'

Everyone laughed, and gathered up their tools, rubbing their hands upon an old piece of cloth that I had brought along for the cleaning. It was now just before nine, and a great thirst was upon us all.

'Let us retire to the tavern once more before the day's work must begin,' declared my husband, and turning to me he added – 'Just one day's watch, Lizzie, and I'll bring you bread and ale in an hour.'

Sin unlocks the gates of Hell.

Thus saying, from her side the fatal key,
Sad instrument of all our woe, she took;
And toward the gate rolling her bestial train,
Forthwith the huge portcullis high up drew,
Which but herself not all the Stygian powers
Could once have moved; then in the key-hole turns
Th' intricate wards, and every bolt and bar
Of massy iron or solid rock with ease
Unfastens ...
    ... She opened, but to shut
Excelled her power; the gates wide open stood...

(Paradise Lost Book 2)

BOOK 2

Now began my most important role in this whole event, and the one that has caused me both the greatest pleasure and the utmost unease in the months since that time, for it led to the present reversal in my fortunes. I was alone in the church, alone save for what was now remaining of England's foremost poet! Imagine my feelings when I thought that everything most precious about the Bard – his head which once contained his fancy, his sunken chest which once contained his passionate heart, his legs – one still intact – which once trod the path of libertie – were now all entrusted to my care! This is a proud day, Elizabeth Grant, I thought to myself, the proudest of your twenty-five years upon this Earth, and you must make sure you prove yourself worthy of the honour which has been bestowed upon you.

I walked about the church to be sure of my charge and to steady my trembling excitement. Even though the sun was by now high in the sky, the stained-glass windows filtered its force so that only a few dusty, dappled beams illuminated the lofty white stone pillars and soaring, pointed arches, turning the old graves and memorials a strange greyish red and blue colour. Passing between the columns, which reach so high towards the roof that it sometimes seems – when you look up – as if they might fall inwards, I inspected all the dark corners to ensure

23

nothing was amiss and nobody was hiding or haunting the shadows. Mrs Hoppey had often told me tales about the church when I was growing up and we were dusting the tombs together, how this was where Oliver Cromwell was married to the daughter of a Cripplegate leather merchant, and where John Bunyon, who wrote *Pilgrim's Progress*, used to worship occasionally, when he was not in prison for being a Dissenter, obviously. And Mr Daniel Defoe, who wrote the books that Mrs Hoppey likes most particularly and was born in Fore Street, was probably baptised in our font and attended the church most of his life.

We were always proud of our history and we knew that many famous men and women had lived here over the centuries and that our church was so old that it must have been built almost at the beginning of time. But now, it seemed to me, we were adding to history ourselves, and that maybe in years to come people would tell the story of us – Grant, Fountain, Laming and the others – and our discovery. You could always read the names of the dead on their graves in the church, but today I had actually looked at the dead, face to face, and seen a famous person in the flesh, not just in a book or carved on a dusty epitaph.

Not long after my husband and the other men left for the tavern, the four workmen arrived to continue their task of repairing the broken flagstones upon the floor. They were initially surprised to see me inside the church, sitting by that time in the council-men's pew beside the pit, with my candle in my hand, although I am a common enough sight outside, digging the graves regular for Mrs Hoppey.

'What is this, you have progressed in the world, Lizzie!' joked the youngest of them, Tom Holland, whom I have known since we played together as children in Fore Street. 'Now you are sitting in luxury inside, instead of toiling under the midday sun!'

'We have done some digging of our own earlier, Tom,' says I, 'and found the greatest prize in Cripplegate, I can tell you!'

The other men stopped laughing and put down their pickaxes,

which they had languidly picked up to begin work.

'The greatest prize! I didn't know we had any worth the mention, Lizzie,' says Tom. 'I know we had to tell Mr Strong yesterday when we came across an old coffin but I did not think that it was anything unusual. Let us have a look then. We can't miss the greatest prize. Come on, show us!'

I sensed that he was still a little sceptical but the men crowded around me, and I took up the candle and lit it, and took them under the pew, and let them peer under the lid of the coffin at the body beneath.

'It's Milton, that is,' says I proudly, as if he were my nearest relation. 'He's a famous poet, the greatest in this country. He's been dead over a hundred years, but he's such a genius that his body can't rot like ordinary people's do. At least, that's what the others told me.'

They were all filled with awe and wonder, that such a revelation could happen in this church, just below where they had been breaking flagstones all these weeks, and they went back to sit beside their present work and talk about the event, taking gulps of gin to assist with the digestion of the news. But I declined to join them – after all, I was commissioned to watch the body and ensure that no unlawful person might enter and presume to touch and damage the sacred remains with no understanding – and I believed that I must keep my sober wits about me.

In a while, Mr Grant brought me a flask of ale, some bread and a large slice of cheese, which I ate with alacrity, having stirred up a good hunger with the morning's actions.

'It is good work that you are doing, wife,' he said to me, as we sat together on the church threshold and watched the street's business going by. 'We cannot afford to leave the body unattended, with the mob wandering the streets, all stirred by unruly passion and lack of care for anything.' He shook his head, for he has been badly stirred by reports of the events in France, and who knows where they may lead? Myself, I think that the day the crowd stormed the Bastille

25

was a fine day indeed, for libertie should be the possession of every innocent man and woman, but Mr Grant has read deeply and knows more about these matters than I.

'Anyway, wife,' said he, 'I must go now to Mr Strong, for there are many letters I must pen and papers I must register today. So guard well the body, and I will come visit you tonight.' And he kissed my brow, and walked up Red Cross Street to clerk business for Mr Strong.

*

My first visitor arrived about an hour later. I was just starting to doze in the mid-morning sun, sitting on the entrance step, my head falling back against the church door, when I felt a prodding at my shoulder. It was Thomas Hawkesworth, who works for Mr Ascough, the coffin-maker, along with Benjamin Holmes. I could remember when he was just a mischievous child in the arms of Mrs Hawkesworth, always grinning and laughing with his wide mouth and sprout of ginger hair. But now he was a tall stripling, cocky and strutting with three years of apprenticeship behind him. He must have been nailing coffins with Benjamin Holmes and heard our news and – always very bold – had come to investigate further.

'I hear the body of a poet's inside,' he nods his head towards the church. 'Give us a view, wench,' says he, with a wink.

I got to my feet and stood between him and the door.

'What's it worth to me?' says I, ever quick to strike a bargain.

'I'll give you tuppence and three kisses,' says he, always the saucy one, though he can be no more than seventeen.

'It'll be sixpence or nothing,' says I, standing my ground. 'It's the greatest bard of England in there, not the poor hole of St Giles'!'

And to my surprise, he slips me a 6d coin just like that (I really don't know where he obtained so much) and I take him past Tom Holland and the other lads, who all look up from their work and make wisecracks about my business, but I just ignores them and leads him to the pit beneath the common-council-men's pew. I stands by as he bends down and pulls the coffin lid back and runs his hands over the strewn remains. I think that he might have found a tooth, which Mr Fountain must have overlooked, for he put something in his pocket, and I fancy I saw him break a little piece of the coffin too.

'What a fine sight!' says he, smiling at me. 'I thank you, Lizzie, for shewing me somebody so famous. And I one of the first to see him! This is a fortunate day indeed!'

And he went out blinking into the sharp sunlight, for there was another coffin to be made that afternoon.

Well, after that I began to get ideas. This Milton could be the making of you, Elizabeth Grant, I tells myself. If every man gives you sixpence for a peek at the remains, there could be a tidy fortune at the end of the night. Why, after only five visitors, you will have collected half a crown! Then I thought some more – if as many as forty two men come, why it will be a guinea you will pocket at the end of the night and then you can buy a new petticoat and a pair of stays and even some fine lace and look quite the lady! And I fell to making all the calculations, thinking of figures and coins and the Cheapside stores and dresses, until my head was reeling and my feet were dancing at the fancy. For although I have a good mind for business, I have a weakness for pretty baubles, and so I was torn this way and that, now logically thinking of sums and money, now giddy with the prospect of delicate cloaths and trinkets.

I was so wrapt up in my thoughts that I did not see my second visitor until he was quite inside the church and bowing low before me. He was dressed in a bright yellow waistcoat, with a large red kerchief half falling from his pocket and a rose in his buttonhole.

'Madam, I pray, conduct me to the threshold where I may view the sacred reliques!' says he in a loud dramatic voice, as if he were in the theatricals and not addressing a mere grave-digger in St Giles'.

'You mean Milton, that was dug up this morning?' asked I.

'Indeed. I wish to pay respects to the dust of that immortal soul,' he replied, and bowed low again, declaring something about fruit from some forbidden tree which I could not understand. I recognised the man now, for it was Mr Ellis of Lamb's Chapel nearby, the comedy actor at the royalty theatre, and I trembled a little, for I had never dared to speak to such a man before. But I kept to my determination and stood my ground between him and the excavation.

'It will cost you sixpence, sir, to go view the body. For it's more than dust, sir. There's hair and legs and more than a few teeth remaining, and I daresay you could even find a finger.' I dropt a curtsey, as low and polite and ladylike as I knew how.

'So the great bard has become the stuff of commerce,' he said sadly. 'Ah me, Mammon is to blame, *Mammon, the least erected Spirit that fell from Heav'n!* And he shook his head, but I thought all the time he was mocking me, for it seemed he did this more for a fancied audience which was not there than for his own sake. He reached deep in his pocket, and drew out a sixpence and said, 'Now wench, be satisfied and shew me the divine vision of Milton!'

So I led him the way to the coffin. But I was a little surprised to notice that, once beside the body, he lost all his grand ways and his dignity which he had assumed on the church threshold, and instead he was more violent than Hawkesworth earlier, breaking off a piece of rib bone with a chisel which he had brought for the purpose and cutting off a clump of hair from behind the ear. He wrapt them both in a paper carefully, and held it under his coat.

'Now not a word about this, wench,' he declared, as we left the church. 'I trust you will not breathe a word about what you have seen,' and he pulled the rose from his buttonhole and offered it to me, with another dramatic bow.

'Of course, sir, not a word,' said I, and stuck the rose in my bosom, where the thorns jostled with the poet's jawbone for the rest of the day.

When he had departed, Tom came up to me, teasing me as he always does but more animatedly than usual.

'Here is too much work on your hands, Lizzie,' says he. 'The men have seen two more visitors heading in this direction, and they reckon that soon there will be more viewers than you can control on your own. I don't underestimate your abilities, Lizzie, but even you, I think, cannot watch over the body alone – and take the money, for we have seen what you are doing. You are pocketing the coins quicker than I can empty a good ale – and I don't blame you neither!'

'A token, Tom, a token,' I murmured, blushing a little, for I did not know my transactions had been noticed. 'It is taking up my time, after all, when I might have been doing other work.'

'True, true, Lizzie, and it will take up much more time, we reckon. The men say that they cannot be concentrating on the flagstones, with all this traipsing to and fro, and so they are proposing to reach an agreement with you.'

'An agreement?' I asked, a little incredulous now.

'That's right,' replied he. 'My men will guard the doors and ensure that each visitor pays you properly for your pains. And in return, they ask only that they can charge each entrant the price of a quart of beer. 'Tis only fair, for managing these customers of yours is going to be hot, thirsty work indeed!'

I thought for a moment, but I could see nothing to my disadvantage in the proposal, and indeed there was much in its favour, so I nodded my assent, and shook Tom's hand firmly. The men all grinned, and put down their tools, which they had hardly used that morning in any case – so distracting was the excitement over the body – and prepared to station themselves around the church, two at the front and one at the side door, leading to the vestry, and the fourth outside, in the yard, to prepare the people for the exhibition ahead.

Well, after this arrangement, it never stopped. I was up and down all day and all the evening too, only finishing the tour with one visitor in time to take the sixpence off the next and conduct him to the pit. They started to form a disorderly line in the churchyard, joking and quipping about the body, and whether it would have rotted away entirely by the time they reached their turn to view it, and others were saying not to worry since at least it wasn't going away anywhere, since it was dead, and then still yet others replied that they on the other hand might die waiting, and could view it in eternity quicker than in St Giles'! At one point, a fight broke out between two men, over who was before the other in the line, and I began to tremble a little at what might be the consequence of what I had started that day, for it was becoming a bigger event than I could ever have expected. But fortunately the workmen ended the fight with a couple of well-aimed blows, and things became quieter and more orderly. The men guarded the door sternly and took their beer money off the punters before they could think twice about it but they made sure that each man paid me the sixpence due, and I thanked them warmly. Even still, a couple of ruffians managed to climb through a window at the back to avoid paying me my sixpence. I found them in the church when I was there shewing the body to John Poole the watch-spring maker, a bent elderly gentleman from Jacob's Passage, whose grandfather, he reminded me, knew Milton when he was old and blind and living in Artillery Walk with his two shrewish daughters. When I saw the villains, who had stolen a peek without paying the entrance, I grabbed the mallet, which Benjamin Holmes had left behind, and gave chase, but they were too quick for me and their feet shot through that window quicker than rats into the sewer.

'That will teach them,' says I to Mr Poole, when I returned. 'They should shew proper respect to the poet.' And he smiled and nodded his head vigorously, placing a toe reverently into his pocket.

By nine o'clock at night, the excitement had died down a little. The number of visitors had diminished, so there was now perhaps only one every half an hour. Maybe most men were abed, or in the taverns, or maybe the word had gone round that there was no longer much of the body to be seen. So frenzied had the viewing been earlier in the day that by nightfall the skull was bald and the hands mere stubs, shorn of all their fingers. The leg bones had disappeared – I never saw who took them – and the chest was all ransacked and empty. The workmen had packed up their tools by now, and departed, shouting and laughing, to spend their day's earnings in Fountain's tavern. I decided to lower the price of entrance to 3d, since there was less to see and very little for the taking, in the expectation that a few of the journeymen who could not afford the 6d during the day might yet pay me 3d for a small share in the spectacle. And they did indeed start to come as darkness drew on, walking softly from the tavern, ashamed to be seen taking an interest in a dead poet perhaps but led on by the thrill of macabre spectacle and the thought – I now realise, although I did not understand this at the time – of the relique trade.

My husband came to visit me around 9.30, exhausted after a long day of writing in Mr Strong's office, in addition to our early morning exertions. Fortunately, there was nobody present to view the body just then, and only Tom stayed on to help me guard the door, so it was not necessary for me to tell Mr Grant the details of my day's business. I met him at the church door and suggested that we just sit down there upon the step, so that he was a considerable distance from the coffin and he would not notice the alteration to the body since he had last seen it that morning. I reassured him that everything was safe and that I was not tired and could manage a couple more hours of the watch.

'Go to your bed, Mr Grant,' said I, stroking his head, where the hair is growing thin and grey, and smoothing his brow, which was lined with care. 'I will wait another hour or two, to do my duty by the poet, and then I will lock up carefully and give the key in to Mr Cole's tomorrow.'

'You're a good woman, Lizzie, England will be proud of what you have done for one of her greatest sons today,' said he. And he walked off home, turning the corner of Fore Street not a moment before Joe Haslib, the journeyman undertaker, appeared from the other direction, dusting a dirty tuppence which was all he could find to give me.

'Just for you, Joe, if you give us a kiss,' said I (for I have always fancied his fresh-faced cheeks), and I lit the tinder-box and led him to the stinking bones.

Heaven awaits while Satan arrives on earth.

Thus they in Heav'n, above the starry sphere,
Their happy hours in joy and hymning spent.
Meanwhile upon the firm opacous globe
Of this round world, whose first convex divides
The luminous inferior orbs, enclosed
From Chaos and th' inroad of Darkness old,
Satan alighted walks.

(Paradise Lost Book 3)

BOOK 3

Now with all these nods and winks and asides about 'I cannot tell you now' and 'more later', I know the time has come to tell the reader something of my former life and of how I came to be married to Mr Grant and of our life together before the day we dug up Milton. I have never told a story before, and my words just tumble out unformed by elegant polish. Indeed I was so carried away with the telling of the events of the fateful night that I quite forgot about what it was rightful that the reader should know first. But now I am corrected and will begin to narrate things in the proper manner.

I was born in the year of our Lord 1765, in a small village near the town of Liverpool in Lancashire. My father was a farm labourer, as decent and hard-working a man as he was poor and simple, and until I had seen seven summers he spent each cold harsh winter ploughing the fields, each spring time sowing the oats and barley and each harvest gathering in the fruit of the year. But the seventh harvest, he received a blow from a scythe which maimed his limbs forever, and rendered him incapable of working on the land ever again. Idle and frustrated, quickly the fortunes of our family slipped through his hands. By this time he had six young mouths to feed, and although my mother earned something taking in washing from the Big House nearby, still there was scarcely enough to support a growing family. Within the year, my father had fallen into debt, and shortly after my eighth birthday the bailiffs came to take him away to gaol.

Imagine the inconsolable grief of my poor mother as she watched her husband led away and looked down at the six sorrowful faces of her children! Once plump and beautiful, she was now thin and pale with the months of anxiety and poverty, although her dark eyes were still deep and soulful and her long hair, now pushed under her threadbare cap, was as yet unstreaked with grey and as lustrous as ever. Never had she wielded a plough or a scythe herself and she knew nothing of the wisdom of farming, having always left that business to her husband to undertake. Uncertain where to turn, she walked up to the Big House to appeal to our landlord, Mr Bullock. I do not know what was said at that meeting, but she visited the Big House many more times following that, and sometimes she had to stay late into the night, talking with Mr Bullock, and my eldest sister, who was ten years old, would give us our dinner without saying a word and send us to our bed.

Maybe my mother's visits to Mr Bullock had a purpose and he was persuaded to help us, because after six months my father returned home from gaol. But I hardly recognised him, so changed was he, all thin and old and weak, with a persistent cough and a fever burning in either cheek. He stayed in bed, coughing all the day and night, and within three months he had died, a tragic loss to all his family.

The anxious care which my mother had expended in tending to my father soon had its direful effect upon her, and within a fortnight she had contracted the pox, and lay dying in the very bed so recently vacated by my father. My eldest sister stayed steadfast at her bedside, wiping her feverish and pock-marked brow until she too contracted the cruel distemper. One by one, all my sisters and brothers fell victim to the dreadful disease, and indeed it seized me too, but with such mild symptoms that I was presently out of danger. Not so my family, and within a couple of months I lost them all, father, mother, sisters, brothers, seven bodies at the undertakers to be mourned!

I was now left an orphan, with my father's elderly aunt my only friend in the world. For I did not consider Mr Bullock a friend, since he had not looked near my family since the day my father came home from gaol and my mother had ceased visiting him at the Big House. My aunt was old and unable to care for me herself, but she was wise, and the day after the funeral of my mother and my siblings, she called me to her cottage to consider what was to be done with me. I had by this age received very little education, since most of my days had been spent helping my father in the fields and then in the last year I had stayed at home with my mother, looking after the baby while she fetched water and heated it for the washing to earn enough to put bread into our mouths. So I could only write my name and read a few words from the Primer that I had learnt at the Sunday school.

My elderly aunt sat in a low box chair beside the smoking fire in her tiny, dark cottage. She made me stand before her, hold out my hands for inspection and curtsey politely.

'Your face,' said she, 'has not been marked at all by the disease, thank the lord.'

And she questioned me most closely about my reading and writing, about which there was very little to say, alas, and about my knowledge of cleaning and tidying and helping around the house. Eventually, she grew satisfied and indicated that I should come to sit close beside her.

'I am most reluctant to lose you, my dear,' says she, 'for I see you are a good girl and a pretty one too. You have your mother's looks. But I have no choice but to send you on, for I can scarcely look out for myself, and besides, I fear that I will not be on this earth much longer.' And she gave another hacking cough, and took a swig from the gin bottle beside her. She continued – 'I have come to this resolution. I have an old acquaintance since childhood who recently has been left a widow and requires assistance. She works as the sexton in Cripplegate in London, now that her husband, the dear lamented Mr Hoppey, has died, and she wrote to me just last month to say that she is looking for a servant to do the housework and help dig the graves on occasion, now that she must do her late husband's work with the burials and all. I will send you to her in London. You must work hard for her, but in return she will care for you and make sure you are properly brought up.'

I assured my aunt of my willingness to accept this plan, and within two days I was in the Chester-Waggon, making my slow progress to the city. It is hard to describe my feelings on this day. How changed was my life! In less than two months I had lost my father, my mother, my five siblings and my family home. I was exchanging the open fields and the small village of my childhood for the vast city of smoke and crowds and noise and hurry, where at that time I knew not a single soul. Yet I was not deterred, friendless as I was, for the novelty of my life and the prospects which I believed the city might hold for me filled my heart with tender excitement. Besides, I trusted my aunt and was certain that in Mrs Hoppey I would find a true friend.

I was not disappointed. Mrs Hoppey proved to be the kindest mistress I could have hoped to find, furnishing me with clothes and food and a small stipend for my work around the house. When she learnt too that I had received very little education, she scolded me and arranged for me to attend the local church school in the Baptist Head Coffee House in Aldermanbury one morning a week, tending to the house herself on those mornings, until I reached the age of fourteen. My early years of neglect, however, must have had an effect on my capacities, for I found that I could never understand words easily and did not manage to progress my reading ability beyond an elementary stage. But arithmetic was another story. The numbers seemed as clear and logical to me as the words were obscure and confusing, and after a few years Mrs Hoppey, recognising my talents, would hand over her accounting for me to undertake, happy in the knowledge that the figures would tally and her burial business would prosper.

So my life continued for ten happy years, as I grew from a young shy child of nine years old to a young woman, plump, strong and healthy, with what men told me was a striking beauty and sparkling eyes. I began to think of Mrs Hoppey as another mother and she was content to think of me as the daughter she never had. She was by then nearly sixty, almost as stout as she was high, and with only two teeth of her own left in her mouth. The two rooms of her house, the closest to St Giles' church, blackened with smoke, were to be kept as clean and tidy as the king's palace, and each day there was to be fresh bread and ale upon the table. But I was always cheerful as I went about my tasks, going early to the market, scouring the stone floor each day, conversing with the other servants at the pump. You, wise reader, may say that the city is dirty and noisy, but for me, growing up, it was as a school-room, where I learnt to stand tall with the other children in the street, to answer with a ready reply quick as the next fellow and to think fast. And once or twice in the year, when I was out walking in Cheapside with my friends, the hawkers and the sweeps and the criers, a shout would go up, and a carriage would rattle by and I would see, in an instant, a lady's face at the window, beauty like a beam of light upon my day.

*

A few days after my nineteenth birthday, my life changed. I was coming back from the market in Milk Street as usual, with my good friend Alice, when Ascough the coffin-maker's boy came running up to me in the street.

'Mrs Hoppey's been taken ill,' cried he. 'She fell down in a faint, and now she's lying out cold on the floor!'

I thought to swoon myself with surprise, but my courage got the better of me and I stood up tall and I says to Ascough's boy, 'Run to

Fountain's, Tom, on Beech Street, and ask him to bring brandy, quick as he can.'

And I hastened to Mrs Hoppey and found her happily conscious again and sitting propped up against the table.

'Reach into the closet, my dear,' said she weakly, 'and you will find my smelling salts.'

I was just starting to administer the salts, when Mr Fountain arrived.

'No need to bother your head with poxy potions!' – shouted he – 'I've got something much stronger as will fortify your spirits!'

And he handed Mrs Hoppey a flask of fine brandy, and she drank it down more greedily than a newborn baby at the teat. He turned and looked at me most intently.

'You look as if you need a swig of this yourself, missie,' says he. 'Put some colour into that pretty cheek again.'

And I took a gulp, and it was like fire going down my throat, and I looked at Mr Fountain as I had never done before. He was about three-and-thirty with a thick auburn head of hair (he wore his real hair then) and ginger hair bristling along what I could see of his strong forearms, sturdy from lifting all the barrels of ale, and with a merry eye. And I blushed and hung down my head, for what reason I could not tell, and he pinched my arm and laughed, a wonderful thunderous laugh, and cried, 'That's what I like to see! A fine maid and proud, with the blood in her veins again!'

After that, Mr Fountain came to visit Mrs Hoppey every day for a week, to ask how she did, and every day he spent more time with me, standing talking as I kneaded the bread and scoured the hearth, and he would slip me a tipple of the same fiery brandy. He would tell me of the gossip from the tavern, about who was up and who was down, about the husbands who were cheating on their wives, and about the other men who were fearful that their women were not honest with them, and he was so humorous that I would laugh despite my best attempt at modesty, and then he would roar with laughter too. I

40

liked his deep voice and his big chest and his wide smile, and when I heard his words as he came to the door – 'How do ye do today, Mrs Hoppey?' – my heart would go aflutter and the colour rush and disappear from my cheek.

On the seventh day, Mrs Hoppey was finally feeling able to walk about again, and being called to assist at a burial, which had been delayed for a few days while she was indisposed, she left me alone in charge of the house for the afternoon. I sat at the table, polishing the pots and feeling most melancholy, dropping a few tears indeed, since I believed that Mrs Hoppey's recovery meant the end of Mr Fountain's visits, when what do you think I heard? Mr Fountain's familiar tread and cheerful cry coming through the house, 'How now, maid, why these tears? Surely your mistress is strong and on her feet again?' And I could not speak but hung my head down lower, and he came and sat beside me, and I think he guessed the reason for my despondency, for he put his arm around my shoulders and said, 'But I shall still continue to see you frequently, if that is to your liking,' and still I could not speak but I nodded my head and he put his fingers to my chin and raised my face and kissed me. And I was so surprised and pleased that I sank down limp in his arms but he held me fast and kissed me again, and I could smell his breath, which was of ale and onions and warm nights.

'You're a charmer, alright, Lizzie, my gal,' he murmured, and we sat together in the kitchen like that, in silence, for once not a quip or a joke between us. I cannot describe my sensations as I lay in my little cot that night, and thought of Mr Fountain and his kiss, but I know it was many hours before my heart was tranquil and sweet sleep came to me.

After that day, Mr Fountain and I were courting, or whatever you want to call it. He would call for me one afternoon a week (most evenings he must attend in the tavern) and we would go walking, under the trees at Moorfields or out to Sadler's Wells, and one special time he

41

even took me to Vauxhall when they had lit over a thousand lanterns. He never once raised the subject of marriage to me, and some nights I grew a little anxious on this score and thought to myself that he meant nothing serious in this attention which he was shewing to me. Perhaps, thought I, there are other women that he sees, for after all, I never went to his house, believing that it was not seemly for me to frequent the tavern, where many different men, and some women of dubious reputation, would drink each evening. But Alice, my closest friend at this time, to whom I confided my secret concerns, assured me that it was known around all the neighbourhood that I was Mr Fountain's favourite girl, and that I was not to be afraid that I had any rival in his affection.

*

Early one evening, we were walking down Fore Street, I holding onto Mr Fountain's arm as he was taking me back to Mrs Hoppey's and thinking all the while, here's another week gone by and still he has not spoken of marriage or if I want to change my name to Mrs Fountain, and only twenty more steps before we must part again with nothing determined between us, when Fountain suddenly stopped and cried, 'Why I do believe, it is Grant! How do you do, sir!' And he took the hand of the man just crossing the street before us and shook it most vigorously. Mr Grant (for it was he) seemed as pleased to see Fountain as he was to see him, and both were slapping each other around the shoulders and smiling and crying.

Then Mr Grant drew up and turned to me, with his eyebrows raised as if to ask Fountain, 'Who is she?' and Fountain stepped back, blushing, and says, 'This is Miss Robinson, Mrs Hoppey's girl,' and Mr Grant asked how I did, and I dropt a curtsey, I don't know why, but he had that effect on me. He was so gentlemanly and polite and also a good many years older than I. Then he said that he must be on his way, and Mr Fountain told him to be sure to call in at his house later, and so we walked on.

'I will tell you his story before we part, Lizzie,' said Mr Fountain, 'for it is a sad tale, but with a happy ending, I have no doubt.'

'I should like to hear it,' said I.

'Mr Grant was born in Beech Street,' says Fountain, 'the only offspring of two elderly parents, and the cleverest child in the neighbour-hood. After just a few months at the church school, the rector of St Giles' picked him for enrolment at Christ's Hospital school. I am six years younger than he but I can still remember, when the rest of us were playing truant, leapfrogging in puddles and chasing marbles and rats in the alley, I would see him, alone in his blue coat, walking down Beech Street with a pile of books under his arm. He was studious all right, and ambitious too, and soon everyone was talking in the street that he was going in for the Law. He became apprentice to a solicitor, and pretty soon was betrothed to the solicitor's beautiful daughter, Lucy Mangan, and Heaven seemed to be smiling upon him.

'It was not smiling for long, however, for the following month old age caught up with his father and he died. His mother could not support the shock and grief of her husband's passing, and in the rapid space of a week she too had followed him. Mr Grant, alone now in the world, was anxious that his training could be speedily brought to a close and that Thomas Mangan would invite him to become a partner in Law. But imagine his horror when he discovered that Mangan had long been engaged in corruption, that his business was entirely sunk in debt and that the bailiffs were coming that very day to lead him to gaol!'

I was, by this stage of the story, so overcome with shock and emotion on hearing the dramatic decline of Mr Grant's fortunes that, without noticing my surroundings, I had pulled Mr Fountain into the churchyard and we were sitting together on a seat there, his arm supporting me as he continued his tale.

'Lucy was now Nathaniel Grant's only care. Motherless since the age of six, she was, with the loss of her father to prison, an orphan, friendless in the world besides Grant.'

'I know only too well what it is to be left an orphan,' I sighed. 'It is a most sorrowful state of affairs, and perilous too. I grieve for Lucy Mangan.' I had confided the narrative of my early life to Mr Fountain during our afternoon walks and so he understood my meaning now and placed his hand tenderly upon my knee in sympathy for a few minutes.

'With Lucy left an orphan,' continued Mr Fountain, 'Mr Grant determined that the best course of action was to go through with the marriage, despite the fact that the prosperity which was to have supported such an alliance had disappeared, and to salvage as much of the business as he was able. So for several years, they lived in his house in Beech Street, while he worked from the earliest dawn light until well after dark, going through the books, writing to the clients and pleading with the debtors. Meanwhile Mangan slowly grew weaker and more despondent in gaol, until in the fifth year of his incarceration he finally breathed his last in Lucy's arms, repenting of all the misery he had inflicted upon his children. Such a loss was not easily to be supported, and Lucy soon took to her bed, sorrow and a rapidly spreading consumption combining to hasten her decline. Grant tended her night and day, his own cares forgotten save for the one meal a day brought to him by Mrs Hoppey. But finally, after a year, all his ministrations could not save Lucy, and she ended her sufferings on this earth, leaving him a widower at eight-and-twenty.'

My tears dropt fast upon my lap now, and I wiped my eyes upon my shawl.

'For sure, Mr Fountain, this is a sad tale indeed, but pray continue, for I tremble to learn what happened next.'

'There was nothing for Mr Grant in the city now,' continued he, 'for he had lost everything – family, wife, employment, fortune. I can remember him sitting on this very seat, ten years ago, shaking his head in disbelief. "Fountain," said he, "nothing is as it seems in this world. You may think that Fortune is favourable, but you see, it is a slippery thing and may leave you like a fickle maid any day." He was, at that time, on the point of moving to the north countries, to try his luck elsewhere. And now he has returned, after ten years of travelling. They say he has been working in the new town of Manchester as a messenger and a clerk and a good many other jobs, and indeed I thought he might have made more of a success of the opportunities there. But it seems that he must have missed his friends in London and that he could not find a good patron or employer up in that foreign town, for he has returned here with not much greater fortune gained than he had when he left. However, he has come down to work as a clerk to Mr Strong, the solicitor, and I dare say he will prosper, because he is prepared to toil many hours and will not be deterred when once he has set his mind to something.'

'Let us hope that now his fortune will follow his obvious merit,' said I, and I trembled a little to think what a fine noble man he was, how unjustified his fate up till now, and how pleased I was to have made his acquaintance.

'Let us hope so, Lizzie,' said Fountain, and as we were in the secluded area of the churchyard, he took the liberty of putting his hand down inside my bosom as he kissed me farewell. But I was not as thrilled as I thought I might be, having waited for this moment a long time, for my mind was still half on Mr Grant and his unfortunate tale.

The following evening, Mr Grant came to visit Mrs Hoppey. He spent an hour sitting at her table, telling her of his adventures up in the north and listening with rapt sympathy as she recounted all her troubles since her husband had died and also of her relief in having me for a servant. I could hear this, for I was mending clothes quietly in the corner, and after this Mr Grant asked me about my family and how I liked it here in the city and I told him everything, although I was a little shy in his presence, because of his great education. But in the following three weeks, he came to visit three more times and on each occasion I became a little less shy, because he was so kind and concerned to hear everything about our lives. He was very different from Mr Fountain. He did not laugh, and he did not possess so merry a wit, and I found that I could not be as natural and rough in his company. But on the other hand, he asked me questions that Mr Fountain had never asked, about my liking for mathematicks and the work on the accounts I did for Mrs Hoppey and about my secret hopes and schemes for life. So it seemed that he was becoming my special friend, someone to whom I could confess things that I had told nobody else.

One Sunday evening, he arrived a little earlier at Mrs Hoppey's and with so serious a manner we wondered what was the matter. He coughed and hesitated a little, and then with a nod of determination, he started to speak.

'Mrs Hoppey and Miss Robinson,' said he, 'I have thought about this matter for many days now and I have come to a decision that it is time to speak. For many years I have been left a widower and although I have often felt the want of that most sweet companionship which marriage provides, I have neither been of sufficient means to propose an alliance with anyone nor found a suitable woman with whom to share life's fortunes. In Miss Robinson, however, I think I have found just such an object of my affection, for I see that she is a sober virtuous young woman, possessed of both intelligence and beauty, and not averse to hard work. So now, if Mrs Hoppey is agreeable, I propose to have her as a help-meet and a companion. And if Miss Robinson, of course, is agreeable too.'

And he bowed to us both, standing there beside the hearth.

I was overcome with surprise and full of confusion, for it was nothing as I was expecting. And I blushed and curtseyed, and ran from the room into the street, and looked over at the seat in the churchyard where just one month before I had let Mr Fountain kiss me. But then I remembered my manners, and I ran back to the house, where Mr Grant and Mrs Hoppey were engaged in earnest conversation, and I dropt another curtsey and said, 'Please sir, excuse my earlier confusion, I am struck dumb with surprise and I know not what to think.'

'It is to be expected,' says he. 'You are young, I am much older and have thought long and hard about these matters. I will say nothing more today, but I will leave the question for your solid consideration, and return again in a week to know your answer.'

And before I had had time to think of a reply, he had made his exit and I was alone with Mrs Hoppey to talk over what had occurred. She of course was most excited, most overcome with Mr Grant's favour, but she knew scarcely anything of my walks with Mr Fountain and could understand little of my heart's affections at the time.

My next meeting with Mr Fountain was the following afternoon. He arrived after dinner to take me for a walk, and we sauntered together to Moorfields, and there was much laughter and jokes as usual, but all the time I was thinking I should tell him of Mr Grant's proposal, and I was feeling nervous and as if a great burden had been placed upon my back and I must drag it up the hill or be defeated. At length, we returned back to Cripplegate, and Mr Fountain took me again to the seat in the churchyard, where we had kissed the month before. We sat there in silence for a minute, and I realised that the moment had come when I must speak, and I felt as if I were standing on the new bridge at Blackfriars and about to leap into the murky, fast-flowing waters below.

'You must know, sir, that Mr Grant has proposed to me, and asked me to be his companion and help-meet, and I must make a decision within the week, and I am at a loss about what I must do.' The words came tumbling out of me.

'Lizzie, Lizzie, you are my girl, what are you thinking?' said he warmly and he pulled me to him and kissed me.

'I know, but Mr Grant is so certain, and I do not know what is the right thing to do.'

'Lizzie, I will show you the right thing to do,' and he took my hand and led me further out of the light, behind the stones in the most distant part of the cemetery. We lay down upon the grass, still with his lips glued to mine, and his hands roving up and down my body, now around my throat, now between my thighs, and now upon the swell of my breasts, which were rising and panting with emotion. He grew more urgent, perhaps with the thought of his new rival, and pushed up my dress and loosed my stays, and I, overcome with the strength of his passion, did not resist but met him with an embrace that I am ashamed now to recall. Being too wound up now to brook a refusal, he unbuttoned and, rolling his thighs between mine, pushed his shaft up into my most tender, intimate parts, which yet were eager to receive him. The pain was immense, yet I stifled my cries, my head on the hard tomb of Thomas Smythe, shoemaker, and my feet curled around the thrusting buttocks of Benjamin Fountain. 'Lizzie, Lizzie,' he kept murmuring, his lips upon my neck and mouth and bare bosom, and his hands holding down my arms into the damp turf. I closed my eyes and abandoned myself to his weight and the movement, the quickening heaves and thrusts which were growing more rapid and violent, piercing right deep inside me until they expired with a shudder and he lay atop me, his thick head of hair upon my shoulder.

We lay a long time in this manner, I looking up at the darkening sky, a few pigeons circling overhead, and he, breathing deeply now, at peace on my shoulder. But then I spoke.

'So when are we to be married, Benjamin?'

He stiffened for a moment, and his breathing stopped. 'Look, I am not the marrying kind, Lizzie,' says he at last. 'I have known three loves in my life, and am still not married at three-and-thirty, so nothing is going to change my mind now. Besides, the tavern is an uncertain business, and not the right life to bring a wife into.'

'What are you saying?' cried I. 'Why are we here? What, do you merely play with me, like a doll?'

'You are my girl now, Lizzie,' says he. 'We are both the same, you and I. We are chancers, adventurers, I can tell. You can help me, I can help you. You should come and work in the tavern. More excitement than serving Mrs Hoppey, I should think.'

But I pushed him off me and cried and cried.

'That was my virtue you have just taken, Benjamin, and now you say I cannot hope for marriage. I may be a servant girl, but I am no whore.'

'Come now, Lizzie,' says he, 'be sensible. You know it is not possible for me to marry you now. My business is going through lean times, but when it is better, in a year or so, then things may be different.'

And he took his neck-chief, and he wiped my eyes, and then he wiped me down between my legs, which were all blood-stained and damp, and he pulled me up to stand beside him, smoothed down my hair, and kissed me once again. And I kissed him back, for I still loved him then, but in my heart I was overwrought with disappointment and anger and bewilderment.

For the next few days, my thoughts were all tumbled into a thousand fragments. I would kneel on the front step, rubbing and rubbing it clean, but all the while I was trying to order my feelings into a tidy shape. On the one hand, I loved Mr Fountain, of that there was no doubt. I felt a deep bond of sympathy in his presence, a tingling in my body when he stood near me, as if all the time I belonged in his arms. But my thoughts were sometimes elsewhere, he could not engage my mind at every level. Besides, he said he could not marry me yet, and what sort of man, thought I angrily, lies with a woman and then tells her, even as his head is upon her chest, that he will not marry her. No, better to go with Mr Grant, who will protect you and care for you, Lizzie, I said to myself. He has been married before, and knows what it is to love and cherish a woman, even in the most difficult of circumstances. He is a wise, good man, and it would be a prudent match. And advantageous, too, I added, for there was no doubting that Nathaniel Grant, who had once been a Blue Coat at Christ's Hospital school, and knew how to read and write and a little Latin besides, and who was starting employment as a solicitor's clerk, was a fine prospect for any servant girl. So I determined upon Mr Grant, but then the thought of my tumble in the churchyard would strike me, and I would become afeard of what it might mean and what Mr Grant would say. I had lost my chastity, and while that normally would not matter if it were to a future husband, since it was to a rival, who was to say what the response would be? So I resolved the matter this way and that, as I cleaned the house, and it was hard to remain calm when Mrs Hoppey asked me each evening how I did, and what was my decision regarding Mr Grant's proposal. Sometimes too, in the dead of night, after I had determined to accept Mr Grant, I thought again guiltily of the hour in the churchyard, of Mr Fountain's groans and thrusts and passionate murmurs, and was filled with an aching, uneasy pleasure.

True to his word, Mr Grant arrived the following Sunday afternoon, and demanded to know my answer. He stood by the door, his coat undone and his neck-chief in a bundle in his fist, which he passed absent-mindedly from one hand to the other as he waited for my reply. I realised with surprise that he was nervous, although I had always thought he was a strong-willed man and so much better than I that nothing I could say would cause him any anxiety or self-doubt. But now I realised that it was as if I held his fate in my hands, and my heart grew tender, looking upon him. He is thinner and more delicate-looking than Mr Fountain, with the lines of care already upon his brow, and he wore an old wig which he had purchased many years before, in his days of greater prosperity, which now he rubbed back and forth distractedly, and I felt that there were practical matters in his dress and his house which he was neglecting and that I could tend to him as he grew older, just as he could teach me many things and support me for the rest of my life.

So I went and stood before him, with my eyes lowered, and said, 'Yes, sir, I do consent to marry you, I wish to be your help-meet and companion just as you say,' and he took me by the shoulders, a broad smile upon his face, and said, 'I thank you most heartedly, Elizabeth, and I vow that you will never live to regret this day,' and he squeezed me and looked into my face, and whispered, 'May I presume to kiss you now?' and I, actually quite bashful because he asked so formally and politely, says quietly, 'Yes, sir, you may do so,' and he bends down and brushes my lips with his so gently it made me feel a little faint, and a warm, tingling sensation rose inside me from below.

We were to be married within the week. Mr Grant was not to be moved upon this point, and I did not feel that I could presume to object, although the speedy onset of married life filled me with not a little trepidation. I suppose that Mr Grant did not want to spend one more week alone than necessity compelled, since it was already ten years since his wife had died, and perhaps he was anxious too to hasten the date of the wedding night, when we would lie together for the first time. But it was precisely the thought of that night which filled me most with dread, for that could be the moment of my unmasking. When he lay with me, Mr Grant would discover that he was not the first to enter me, and that I was already undone. Whenever I thought upon that possibility, I grew most weak indeed and I was almost tempted to cancel the whole affair, but Mr Grant was so determined, and Mrs Hoppey was all smiles and excitement the meanwhile, dancing around the kitchen as if she were a giddy girl of twenty again and baking every night between burials, so there was nothing I could do to prevent it.

The wedding was held in St Giles', right over where we dug up Milton six years later, and there was a party afterwards at Mrs Hoppey's, which spilled out into the street so crowded was it, since everyone from the parish was there. Mr Fountain provided the ale, which was extremely generous of him, since he had not spoken a word to me since the rumour had reached him that I had accepted Mr Grant.

51

But Mr Grant was his old friend, and Mrs Hoppey his neighbour, so people would have thought it very strange if he had not been present and acting the life and soul of the party as usual. He was quieter than normal, however, and I thought he was going to say nothing to me at all, but as I was in the back, collecting extra cups since more people had arrived, he caught me by the arm and drew me into the corner.

'Why are you doing this, Lizzie?' said he, pulling hard on my arm. 'You know I love you passionately.'

'You say that, Benjamin,' whispered I, 'but you cannot offer me marriage – A tavern girl is no life for me!'

And I pulled away my arm, and walked back to the party where my husband – I could say that now, after one hour of marriage! – was standing talking and helping old Joseph and Mary Jewkes to a seat. I touched his arm, and handed him the cups for their ale, and stood by his side, while Mr Fountain, I imagine, was still lingering in the back room, to think over what I had said.

The night came, bringing the climax of my fears. Mr Grant had taken me to his house nearby in Beech Street, and led me gently to the bed. It was only eight days since I had lain with Mr Fountain in the churchyard, and the memory of his violent embrace was still strong within me and I trembled to think of what must happen now and how I must behave. But Mr Grant took that trembling to be my maidenly fear and so he lay down beside me and stroked my body carefully, not applying pressure or forcing himself upon me. And so I grew calm, and in time tender, until I began to stroke him in return, and we clung to one another, he placing light kisses all over my face and neck, and I rubbing my face against his in return, so that I scarcely noticed when he entered me, so warm and kind was it, and I forgot to pretend to be shocked or not to be shocked, or to feign bashfulness, or all the other tricks I had fancied beforehand, because I was overcome by a new sort of love and could be directed only by him. Afterwards, I lay in his arms, and my mind was clearer then, and

I was waiting in fear for him to say something, such as, 'So you have known another, Lizzie,' or, 'Where is the stain of your maidenhead?' or – worst – 'You whore, I see you must have rolled with many a man in the past already.' So I was lying there, my heart beating fast, ready to be driven out into the street after only seven hours of marriage. But he said nothing. He said nothing at all. I was waiting, but not a word came. To this day, he has never asked me about my past nor about Mr Fountain. I scarcely knew whether he was very foolish or very wise. He reads a great many books, and maybe he had read that there are other virtues in a woman besides her chastity, or maybe he thought that his silence was the greatest punishment he could inflict upon me, for it has caused me many hours of confusion and guilt in the years since, but at the time I could only lie and think, this man is the wisest and most merciful man alive, and I am the luckiest woman to have him for a husband. Make yourself worthy of him, Elizabeth Grant, thought I, my heart racing to use that name already.

*

I was brought to bed with child nine months later, and I still know not to this day whether this was the late child of Mr Fountain or the early child of Mr Grant. For the boy lived only two days, a poor weak thing, and then he died when it was too early to identify his characteristicks. I was ill for a month with the fever, too ill to attend the child's funeral, and so I was never able to look upon his face closely and decide if I saw Mr Fountain's sparkling eyes there or Mr Grant's worried intelligence. But I was sure, in my heart, that the boy was Fountain's, for why else would the Lord allow him to die unless as a punishment for Fountain and me, for our licentiousness and unlawful ardour. And so I lay in my delirium, thanking the lord for delivering me from the shame of bringing a bastard child into the world, whom Mr Grant would have recognised in due course was not his own, but also at the same time bemoaning the power that allowed such an innocent soul to be unjustly snatched away, because of my sins, before he had had time to receive the love and care that I had been ready to bestow upon him.

It may be too that the child was Fountain's, for in the years since, no further child was born to Mr Grant and myself, despite many months of lying together and enough love and esteem between us to produce twenty babies. Two miscarriages I suffered over the following couple of years, but after that our marriage was barren. We worked together, I keeping the accounts for him and Mr Strong, and he reading to me each evening and writing any letters I must send to our creditors. But there was a silence between us, about my past and about our future, since I could not raise the subject of my former life or my secret feelings of guilt, and we had not created any physical proof of our love or legacy for our old age.

Satan plots the temptation.

One fatal Tree there stands of Knowledge called,
Forbidden them to taste: knowledge forbidd'n?
Suspicious, reasonless? Why should their Lord
Envy them that? Can it be sin to know,
Can it be death? And do they only stand
By ignorance, is that their happy state,
The proof of their obedience and their faith?
O fair foundation laid whereon to build
Their ruin! Hence I will excite their minds
With more desire to know, and to reject
Envious commands, invented with design
To keep them low whom knowledge might exalt
Equal with the gods...

(Paradise Lost Book 4)

BOOK 4

The following morning, after my fateful day exhibiting Milton's body, Mr Grant was up out of bed and had left the house for Mr Strong's before I had even wakened, so tired was I from my previous evening's exertions. He had already been snoring when I returned home the night before, and so I was able to wrap the jawbone carefully in my best petticoat and slip it among my intimate garments, without any awkward questions being asked. I was not conscious of any strong feelings of guilt concerning my activities of that day. Indeed, I was proud of the role that I had played in the historical event and the alacrity with which I had noticed the opportunity for business, and I felt excited when I thought of the money I had earned, which was now safely hidden in my petticoat beside the bone. But on the other hand, when I saw Mr Grant peacefully sleeping without a care, I knew that for some reason he would not approve of my work, and so I felt relieved that I would not be prevailed upon immediately to confide the source of my private exhilaration. I therefore crept into the bed silently beside him, and lay there with my thoughts still whirling, about the discovery and the fame and the money, and it must have been more than an hour before I could abandon myself to the ease of sleep.

I was singing cheerfully and rolling out pastry in the mid morning for a steak pie (Mr Grant is extremely partial to pies, and I wanted to cook something special, by way of private celebration), when Mr Fountain came to the door, even redder in the face than usual and panting for breath. He was not accustomed to call very often, judging it best, no doubt, to keep some formal distance between my marital home and himself, so I was greatly surprised to see him and began to fear some dreadful event had occurred.

'I have just come from talking with Haslib's boy, Joe,' he began, throwing himself down on the chair before me and drawing himself up to the table, without even bothering with all the formal preliminaries of how I did or how was Mr Grant or how hot was the weather. 'I have just been talking with Joe Haslib and he told me something which caused me some unease and which I think only you can solve, Lizzie.'

'Why, how does the matter relate to me?' cried I, innocent as a newborn, although my heart was racing and for the very first time I felt a pang of shame. I added a little more flour to the pastry and rolled it again to hide my confusion from Fountain. But he was scarcely noticing, so wrapt up with what he had to say was he. He leant forward, pushing up his sleeves, and raised his voice a little more.

'Haslib,' said he, 'is engaged at this very moment in cutting up Milton's rib bones into small pieces with the intention of selling them at a profit. Joe told me that he saw his father this very morning, with a file, sawing the bone into one-inch fragments. "Why, that's impossible" – says I to Joe – "Only six people were present when we opened the coffin yestermorning, and Mrs Grant watched it carefully the rest of the day". "Surely you know what later ensued?" – says Joe – "The whole neighbourhood flocked to see the spectacle and touch the body. Why, I myself came away with a small memorial" – And he pulled out a dirty tooth, Lizzie, from his pocket to show me. I knew not what to say to him, so I have hurried straight here to find out the veracity of this story. Surely it is not true that all these people have gained access to the corpse?'

I stopped rolling and wiped the flour off my hands. It was difficult to know what to say, since pride and fear about the consequences of my actions were gripping my heart in equal measure.

'Indeed it is true, Benjamin,' I whispered. 'A couple of men came, having heard about our discovery and wanting to view the body, and I thought, what is the harm in showing them the remains of the finest poet in England, so I took them to the place, but I was not going to accept nothing for my pains, so I demanded a small charge.'

'Gracious heavens, Lizzie, what did you charge?' says he, his hand gripping my arm. I had sat down at the table beside him by this time, and was shuddering with the telling of the tale.

'I demanded sixpence, and the men were happy to pay it,' says I, and I flushed briefly with pleasure at the memory of those coins wrapped in my petticoat. 'So I showed one after another to the coffin under the pew with the help of my candle, until well after it grew dark, and all were most delighted with what they had seen and most grateful to me for enabling it. It was a busy day, Benjamin' – here I sighed dramatically – 'and I am well weary today, I can tell you!'

'But, tell me, Lizzie,' says he, 'how is Haslib sawing up Milton's ribs, if you only took the people to look at the body?'

'It may be' – says I, blushing a little now – 'that a few broke off a piece of the body, as well as touching it with respect. I did not question them on this matter, for it seemed to me that they had paid a large price, and were entitled to some souvenir of their visit. Besides, what is the harm done in taking a little fragment? After all, we took away something earlier in the morning.' And I flashed him a big, conspiratorial smile in the hope this would soften his temper.

'The harm' – says he firmly (and I remember this most distinctly, for it made a strong impression on me at the time, appealing as it did to my economic frame of mind) – 'the harm is that it has seriously undermined the value of our treasure. Here I thought that only six people in the world were honoured to possess a little piece of Milton, and to this end, I took very little in the morning, thinking that the scarcity of the memorials would increase their price. But now I hear that Haslib, and maybe half of Cripplegate, is currently in possession of most of the skeleton, and is at this moment preparing it for the market. And my paltry handful of hair, which yesterday had a rare value, is today of slight regard when any man may purchase a whole leg bone for the asking!' And he banged his fist down upon the table, in anger at the injustice of the situation.

I had to think quickly now, for it had never occurred to me before, that my considerable reward for showing all these people to the body had actually been to Mr Fountain's disadvantage. And to Mr Grant's disadvantage, I added to myself, for my husband himself had taken some hair, although I did not know for certain whether he was intending to sell it.

'I am very sorry that I did not realise the consequences of my actions yesterday,' says I, 'but I think that the situation is not irredeemable. Mr Grant told us that Milton's hair was one of the most remarkable features of his person, so it may well be that it will fetch a higher price than a similar size piece of rib or leg bone in any case. You took a sizeable amount of hair, did you not, Benjamin?'

'Yes, I did, Lizzie,' he nodded. 'For I had taken a few strands, but then after Grant plunged his hand in, I realised the importance of the hair and seized a whole handful more.'

'Well, then,' says I, 'might we not carefully wash it and cut it, and prepare it in small packets for sale? I can assist you in this, for Mr Grant is busy at Strong's for the day, and once this pie is cooking, I have some spare time.'

'That will help a little, Lizzie,' says he, 'but Haslib probably is already selling his bones and catching the best customers. And besides, most of the customers will not know one piece of Milton from another, and who among them will say that the hair is more valuable than the ribs? They will be persuaded by Haslib to part with their money for a bone, and most of them will rate that higher than a lock of hair, and will have no coins left for my market in any case.' And he looked melancholy again, and as if he might make some further violent gesture.

I thought a little more. There was my jawbone, hidden in my petticoat, which I had wanted to keep especially for myself, because Fountain had given it to me, and it affected my emotions in ways that I could not explain. But now here was Fountain most troubled because he had no bones of the Bard to sell, and I was indirectly the cause of his anxiety. I made a quick decision.

'I still have the jawbone which you gave me,' says I. 'We could chop that up for sale too. Let us go into partnership, sell the bone and hair for a shilling a-piece. I reckon you could get ten cuts from that bone at least.'

'Thank the Lord, I knew you had some spirit!' shouts Mr Fountain, leaping to his feet and whirling me around the room. 'We will show old Haslib that he is not the only crafty salesman in the area. A hair and jaw package will be something to be reckoned with. And I think, you know Lizzie' – and he stopped still, his face more serious now as he attempted to make his calculations – 'we could get as many as fifteen cuts from that bone, if I remember it correctly, and could ask 1/6d for each too. It could mean a fortune of –' and here he broke off, for mathematicks have never interested him as much as good conversation and beer.

But I touched his arm, and whispered – for I was ashamed to voice my desire any louder – 'I do wish, Benjamin, to keep a little of the jaw back for my own.' He looked puzzled and slightly disappointed, although the reason for my wanting to retain the bone was on account of my secret liking for him, even now I was married, which I could not confess. So to make amends I continued with a further scheme of my own.

'But I have been considering our plan further, and I think that there is one other strategy we could adopt. Our difficulty, as you say,

61

is that most of the people living around here, who are the most likely to buy the bones, do not know anything about Milton, save that he is a famous poet and a patriotic Englishman, so they will probably prefer to buy Haslib's sturdy ribs or another man's piece of shank, rather than our more delicate jaw or lock of hair. It seems to me, therefore, that we need to sell our fragments to the educated classes, who will appreciate them for what they are and value them accordingly. We need to find men like Mr Grant, or even more educated, who have read Milton and will want to spend a good sum of money buying an important piece of him.'

'By heavens, I never realised before what a clever girl you are, Lizzie!' shouts Fountain. 'What an excellent idea! We need to find customers outside Cripplegate, who will pay us what this hair is worth! Let Haslib and others concern themselves about the small folk around here, who might pay 10d for a splintering bone. We can think bigger, we can draw in the people who matter.'

'But how do we do that?' I asked, for it seemed to me that we could talk grandly but the task of actually communicating with the educated classes was well nigh impossible, since I had never spoken to one in my life (saving, of course, Mr Grant and Mr Strong).

'I'll give it some thought,' says Fountain. 'I am sure that I will find a way. Do not worry about it. In the meantime, fetch me that jawbone and I will take it away to cut it up.'

I looked a little concerned about this, for I had wanted to be present for the chopping, since it was my bone. But he pinched my cheek and smiled.

'Cheer up, Lizzie, don't be anxious, I'll take good care of your bone. And you've your pie to bake now. We can't leave old Nathaniel Grant going hungry because of Milton, now, can we?' And he laughed loudly, and so I laughed too – it felt for a moment like the old days before my marriage – and I ran to my chamber and unwrapped the bone carefully and placed it into Mr Fountain's hands.

*

After I had finished baking my pie and fetching the water from the pump and hanging out the day's washing, I calculated that I had still a couple of hours in which I could safely visit Mr Fountain before Mr Grant would return home for his dinner. Alice, my friend and Mr Strong's maid, had come running to me from Red Cross Street at midday to tell me that my husband would be working late there, because there was an important law case which needed to be prepared and several hours of work had been missed the day before because of his late start. I think that my husband could not have informed Mr Strong about the reason for his late arrival the previous morning, probably because of some anxious fear that Mr Strong would not be pleased to hear of our excavation, but what he did tell him I do not know, since we had had no opportunity to discuss the day's events. No doubt it was some tale about his carousing at Fountain's and his deep slumber and sore head the following morning, and his shocking inability to arise from his bed before nine. Mr Strong would have looked disappointed but stoically patient and my husband would have added his own private feelings of guilt, regarding the real cause of the tardiness, to his assumed shame about his drunkenness that he was projecting for Mr Strong.

It was always a delicate matter, my husband told me, working for Mr Strong. For Strong was not so clever as Grant, but he had been born, the only child, to ambitious parents who poured all their money and attention into the rearing of their son. So that, although they were only publicans, with very little education themselves beside simple reading and writing, they managed to pay for their son to attend St Paul's school, and later to be apprenticed to a solicitor in Holborn. Now as the only solicitor in Cripplegate, he had an inclination to self-importance, since there was scarcely anybody else in Red Cross

Street (except my husband) with as much education and nobody else with as much money (except, no doubt, Mr Whitbread but he kept himself to himself and we knew nothing of him). Strong was possessed of a sociable air and winning smile and always had a hand ready to reach in his pocket to shower a few coins into the grateful lap of a needy neighbour, but I had noticed that he always took the front pew in the church and made sure that people were aware of all his acts of generosity. He would walk the streets with a stick – he was no more than three-and thirty – and nod his head in greeting to everyone he met, his delicate wife hanging on his arm, and their two burly children following with their nurse behind. They seemed the perfect family, but I knew that in fact Mr Strong could be narrow-minded and vain. It was his secret ambition to become a common-council-man, and so he made himself apparently amenable and indispensable to those in the parish he believed possessed authority and influence. With my husband, he was amicable and apparently open, treating him for the most part as an equal (which indeed he was, or even Mr Strong's superior, for he had enjoyed as much education and was a good deal more clever, but he had fallen upon ill times). Mr Strong needed him for his knowledge of the law and his good judgement, but he would always seek opportunities to remind my husband subtly that he was merely the clerk and that he, Mr Strong, was the upright solicitor, without whom the moral order of Cripplegate could not be maintained. My husband's supposed excess of drinking, therefore, and his morning headache from over-indulgence, must have been seized upon by Mr Strong as an example of his inferiority, and although he would not have said anything beside shaking his head sadly, my husband would have felt the full weight of his disapproval. I could picture him in my fancy now, not rising from his desk for hour after hour, dipping his pen into the ink and scratching it across the paper, his old wig tossed on a chair beside him and his hand occasionally rubbing the few hairs that still sprouted upon his worried brow.

My heart grew tender for a few minutes as I thought of Mr Grant, hunched over the desk, copying document after document to make amends to Mr Strong, but then I remembered my jawbone, which Mr Fountain might at that very moment be chopping up, and so I threw my shawl about my shoulders, and trotted along to his house on the corner.

There was nobody in the taproom at the front, but I made my way through to the little back parlour and there I found Mr Fountain sitting at the table, surrounded by files and hair and fragments of bones. He was engaged in trying unsuccessfully to tie a bundle of hair together with an old ribbon. He leapt up when he saw me, spilling the parcel's contents over the table, and seized me by the shoulders, swinging me around until my feet knocked against the table and nearly swept the bones flying across the floor.

'Lizzie' – cries he – 'I am so pleased that you are here! See I am trying to tie up these bundles for sale, like you suggested, but my fingers are not nimble enough and the hair keeps slipping out of the loops of the ribbon.'

Mr Fountain does, indeed, have very large hands, as broad as coal shovels, with fingers thick enough to plug a beer barrel but no use in the finer arts of needlework or craftsmanship.

'Pshaw, Benjamin,' says I, 'you should have waited for me to arrive and not attempted to fiddle with these ribbons, for this is delicate work and better fitted for women's hands.'

'I wish I could wait, Lizzie,' says he, 'but the word reached me at midday that Haslib's bones are already being sold on the streets. Why, one strange man, not from these parts, who came into my house today to buy a pot of ale, had bought a piece of bone off him. He took it out to show me. A piece of leg bone, he told me. Naturally I asked him how he heard about the matter. "Well", says he, "my boy was down at the Clerkenwell pump this morning, and got talking to Haslib's boy. A great poet's parts are going for the asking, he was told, if you travel down to Cripplegate today". So he took his savings and hurried down here, and bought this off Haslib for a couple of shillings. "It took a bit of finding, mind you", says he, "for Haslib's house is not well marked and everyone in the street was a little reserved and suspicious of my enquiries". So, Lizzie, after this, I became anxious again, and as soon as it was possible, I closed the tavern and hurried in here to prepare our reliques for market. There is no time to lose. For what chiefly concerns me is something else which this stranger told me.'

'Why, what was that?'

'He told me that he planned to cut up the piece of leg bone which he bought from Haslib and sell the smaller pieces for a shilling each, to make a profit, right across Clerkenwell. The market is spreading, and we will have less and less influence upon it, I fear.'

And at this, he began washing more clumps of hair feverishly, pouring water from the bucket over them and rubbing them in his hands.

I touched his arm to calm him down. 'Never fear, Benjamin,' says I. 'These lumps of bone will not look anything. Our product, on the other hand, will look the most attractive and valuable on the market.'

And I sat down and began to sort out the muddle heaped upon the table, into small orderly piles, each with a piece of jawbone and a few locks of light-brown hair, which I carefully combed. I demanded that Mr Fountain go to find some pretty cloth or soft flannel, that we might wrap each delicate pile together into a precious parcel, and he was happy to oblige, more tranquil now that there was somebody else to organise this difficult operation. While he was briefly absent from the room, a strange fancy seized me – I know not from where – to slip one of those pieces of the jawbone into my bosom, where the whole had originally been secreted. What I thought to do with the piece I had no notion, but I desired once again to have a relique of my poet (for so I now thought him) close by my side.

When Mr Fountain returned with the cloth and ribbon, I had resumed organising the piles of remains. Then I cut up the cloth into four-inch squares, placed the hair and bone fragment inside each, and rolled it up, fastening it with the browning ribbon, tying it beautifully with a bow just as Mrs Hoppey had taught me. So after one hour and a half, there were thirty elegant packages lined up on Mr Fountain's table, as gaudy and exciting as anything in the storefront windows in the Chepe.

'You are a wonder, Lizzie!' says Mr Fountain, gazing down upon the afternoon's work. 'This is worth any number of leg bones. Why, I declare, all the ladies in London will be lining up to buy these parcels!'

And he put his arm about my shoulder and gave me a squeeze, and – I must confess – a quick peck on the cheek. But I, feeling a little awkward on account of Mr Grant being unaware of what was going on, moved a little apart and put on a serious air.

'We must think, Benjamin, what it is therefore correct to charge for each package. If Haslib's selling his leg fragments for two shillings a piece, I reckon this is worth at least that amount.'

'You're right, Lizzie,' says Fountain. 'What say you to 2/6d?'

'We can try that, at least,' I replied. 'For we can start at that price, and if they are not selling, then we will have to drop the figure.'

'Excellent plan,' says he. 'I will keep them here, and then if anyone comes to the tavern asking about Milton or the bones or Haslib or any such similar matter, I shall slip them the word and make the transaction quietly around the back.'

'Yes, Benjamin, I think that is best. For you will meet many such customers in your house. But be sure' – and here I ventured to touch him upon the arm to emphasise my point – 'be sure to divide the profit equally with me. For I reckon that this could earn us a total of 75 shillings, if all goes well.'

'Do not worry, Lizzie,' he whispered. 'We are in this together, we are a team, you and I, as I have always said.' And he pressed his lips to mine, to seal the pact.

I was anxious to leave now, to go home to prepare the house for

Mr Grant's return, but Mr Fountain insisted that I drink a pot of ale with him to toast our promised fortunes. So I somewhat reluctantly agreed, swallowing the drink in five long gulps in my haste, and running back along Beech Street to my house, feeling as if I were floating like a giddy raft upon the strong brew and the romantic excitement and the high hopes for imminent riches.

*

When Mr Grant returned home that evening, he looked weary enough to wring out in a mangle. His brow was furrowed and his cheeks were grey, and his thin bony fingers were covered with ink stains and smudges.

'Sit down, Mr G,' said I, bringing his night cap and his slippers, 'and I will bring you a mug of ale and some pie by and by.'

'O Lizzie,' said he, hunched at the table with his head in his hands, 'Mr Strong will push me too far one of these days. Here I have been, for ten long hours, poring over the papers for errors and copying out the letters for all the creditors with scarcely a bite to eat or drink and no step outside into the daylight, and then in the last hour, when I am completing my pile and preparing to leave, Mr Strong comes through with another message he must dictate which must be copied and sent to six different recipients!'

My husband groaned at the memory, and took off his boots, and sat in exhausted silence for a few minutes, dangling and wriggling his toes in the warm evening air.

'Take heart, Mr G,' says I, 'and have a good rest now. See, I've baked you a steak pie.' And I put the pie down in front of him, with some steaming leaks and a good bottle of ale beside it too.

'Well, this is a wonderful sight indeed!' said he, and he served himself a large plateful, and ate his way through, telling me, all the while, about Mr Strong and the letters and the long day's work.

From this, I discovered that he had heard nothing at all about the cutting up of the bones and the sale of Milton's reliques, since he had been inside Mr Strong's house all day and not been privy to the gossip in the street. He did ask me a little about my vigil over the body the day before, and how I had found the strength to continue well into the night, after he had been compelled to retire to his bed. But I told him simply that the workmen had kept me amused with conversation during the day, and that I had been sustained as well by the knowledge that I was charged with an important task and that he and Mr Laming and Mr Fountain and the other men depended upon me. I did also confess to him that a few visitors had stopped by the church – I thought it best to give him as honest a tale of my day as possible – and that I had taken it upon myself to shew a few of them to the coffin, for they had expressed such a desire to see it and who was I to prevent them, if they were upright people and serious about their intentions towards the poet? But for some reason, which I could not quite explain to myself at this time, I decided not to tell Mr Grant about charging them sixpence to see the body, and I certainly did not tell him about people breaking off little pieces of the body or the coffin as souvenirs. I did not deem these actions immoral at this time, but still I had an innate sense that Mr Grant would not approve.

After dinner, he could not stay awake any longer – indeed his head was sinking towards his plate during the last few mouthfuls – so I helped him to his feet and led him to the bed in the back-room, where he sank down gratefully and almost instantly fell into a deep, peaceful slumber, for once too deep even to snore.

But, despite my exertions of the last two days, I was not tired at all, but rather caught up in a tremulous mixture of anxiety and excitement as I thought about our parcels and the possibility of the sale. In chief, I was most eager to know whether Mr Fountain had sold any of the packages of hair and bone, and so, as it was not yet dark, being a hot summer night, I decided to venture out and run to Mr Fountain's, to ask whether he had yet met with any success.

I was reluctant to walk straight into the taproom, for it was well into a Thursday evening by that time, and all the tradesmen in the area were drinking hard, near the end of their week. But fortunately Mr Fountain saw me loitering at the entrance, and signalled for me to meet him around the back. He was most excited.

'Lizzie, I have sold five parcels already!' he whispered, as soon as I was within earshot. 'Five parcels, at 2/6d each! The customers are starting to hear about our collection, and they slip me the nod over their porter.'

'Who are these people?' I asked him. 'How did they hear about it? Why are they buying our remains, rather than Haslib's?'

'I cannot tell,' he replied. 'I have not recognised any of them. They are not from our street, that is for sure. Perhaps the word has spread at least to Clerkenwell.'

'Well, that is good news,' says I. 'It means over 12 shillings already, in a few hours.'

'Yes, but that's not the best news. The last man to buy the hair from me this evening was a writer from Grub Street, not five minutes from St Giles'. He publishes his writing in a newspaper, though I forget the name now.'

'Which newspaper, Benjamin?' I asked him crossly. 'Try hard to remember, for this is important.'

'Yes, indeed,' he replied, 'for this man told me that he thought his paper would be interested in the story. At least, he said he would speak to the general editor of the newspaper in the morning. He asked me various questions, about how we found the body and how we knew it was Milton and what was the state of the corpse now.'

'So, what did you tell him?'

'The truth, of course, Lizzie,' whispers Mr Fountain. 'I told him everything as I could remember it. He wrote a few words down as I was speaking, in a small notebook that he pulled from his pocket.'

'No doubt he will publish the story in the newspaper,' says I, a little anxious now, for there was no saying for certain what Mr Fountain had told him.

'Of course, Lizzie,' says Mr Fountain, in a loud, excited whisper now. 'This is what we wanted, is it not? For now the news will spread all over London, and the more educated classes may read of it, and know that Milton's hair is there for the buying, and we can charge yet more for our parcels.'

'Let us hope that is the case, Benjamin,' said I. 'It would be very good if you could remember the name of the newspaper, so that we can try to buy a copy (with our new profit from the hair sales) and read what has been written.' And then I blushed a little, for I knew that I could not read newspapers very easily, and that I must ask either Mr Grant or Mr Fountain to read the article for me.

'I think,' said Mr Fountain at last, walking round and round the empty barrels in his backyard in the effort to trace back the coils of his memory, 'it was the something Advertiser.'

'It must be the *Public Advertiser*,' says I, recalling that this was a favourite paper of Mrs Hoppey's. She would sit for hours reading each line carefully, including even the advertisements for boot polish. 'I like to follow the fashions' – she would say to me with a wink and a grin – 'I need to know who is being buried and who is being hanged, and what the doings are in the theatres.' So now I mentioned the name to Mr Fountain.

'The very same!' declared he. 'I will buy it on Saturday and tell you what it says.'

Then – I tremble to say this, but I must confess everything that happened in these few fateful days – he put his arms about me and pushed me up against one of the barrels, his hands roving beneath my skirts. And I did not resist, but even assisted him, pulling off his shirt and tugging him urgently towards me. We fell back among the old ale caskets, and rolled over and over, between the unused ribbons and scrap material, clinging and panting and groaning as loud as we would dare. It was the first time I had erred in six years of marriage. Maybe it was the heat or maybe it was the fact that I had spent more time alone with Mr Fountain in the last two days than I had in all my married life. Maybe even it was the excitement of the business we were creating together. In any case, I clung to him passionately in the sticky night air and his sweat showered my face and chest in a thousand droplets, and afterwards we lay exhausted, a tight hot ball of damp bodies, united in desire and guilt.

It was sealed. We had a deal. And so I clambered to my feet, wiped myself down with a tavern towel and ran back along Beech Street, besides the shadowy almshouses, concerned to get back inside before it was completely dark and before Mr Grant might waken and miss me.

Adam comforts Eve.

Evil into the mind of god or man
May come and go, so unapproved, and leave
No spot or blame behind: which gives me hope
That what in sleep thou didst abhor to dream,
Waking thou never wilt consent to do.

(Paradise Lost Book 5)

BOOK 5

The first time I heard the name Milton I was walking across Bunhill Fields burial ground with my friend Alice. Her father had died but a month before, after a cruel and lingering illness throughout which Alice, his sole surviving child, had cared for him tenderly and selflessly. Now alone, her mother having died in childbirth, she had been compelled to go into service and was just commencing work for Mr Strong's new bride, who was with child, though Alice was scarcely more than a child herself. But always cheerful and resourceful, Alice had comported herself most impressively in her first week, with the consequence that Mrs Strong had said that she might 'go to visit her father's grave' one afternoon, when she could manage without her for a couple of hours. So Alice had called for me at Mrs Hoppey's, and I was glad to link my arm through hers and sing our favourite ballads together to raise our spirits as we walked along Artillery Walk northwards to Bunhill.

The grave of Alice's father was easy to find, since it had been so recently dug and the grass had not yet begun to sprout upon the reddish-brown clay soil. A headstone was as yet beyond Alice's pitiful means but we gathered pebbles from around the corners of the burial ground and added some buttercups and pansies, so that after less than an hour we had such a fine heap of stones and flowers upon the earthy mound that I declared that it looked finer than any polished monument. Alice shed some more tears at that point, mainly, as she said, because she was happy that her father's life was now marked with our frail memorial. And then we jumped up and ran between the graves, trying to outrun and catch the other, for we were but thirteen years old and still children in our hearts.

As we were coming out of the gate of Bunhill, laughing and panting for breath, Alice looked across at one of the houses opposite and said that it was house of Mr Milton.

'Who is Mr Milton?' asked I. 'I have not seen him at church or heard tell of him in the streets.' I could only think of the corn mill near Liverpool, where we had taken the grain to be ground after each harvest when I was a child. My father would load up the cart with mounds of our freshly cut oats and I would clamber up to join him, sitting between his strong legs as he held the reins and looking between the horse's ears as we bumped slowly over the rough ground towards the mill. Now, of course, a new cotton mill is built nearly every month it seems in Lancashire (so Mr Grant tells me) and manufacturing cloth is often undertaken by machines, not people, in new and growing mill-towns, but back then, when Alice said the word Milton, immediately a picture of the large, creaking wooden wheel moving by the power of the river water and grinding our season's grain flashed into my mind.

'Milton is dead, Lizzie, you fool,' laughed Alice. 'He died more than a hundred years back. But this is where he lived, close to Bunhill.'

'But why do you tell me this? Who was he or why do you recall him now?'

'I know,' says Alice, 'that he was a very great man, one of the greatest men in Cripplegate. My father used to speak of him. His father told him that *his* grandfather had sometimes run messages for Mr Milton when he was a boy. He was a stern man, quite severe, with little patience, he said, but he had a great liking for the Idea of the people, and for Freedom.'

'What is the Idea of the people?" I asked. 'People are human, are they not? They are not ideas, like the minister tries to fill us with every Sunday in his sermon. They are real people, like you or me or Mrs Hoppey or Mrs Strong.' And at that point I let out a shout, because I remembered that we must both be back soon to help Mrs Hoppey and Mrs Strong prepare dinner and they would be waiting for us and if we were late we would never be able to see each other and go walking together again. So we ran back hurriedly and did not talk about the subject any further.

But my curiosity had been raised and my thoughts not a little confused by Alice's comments and so that evening, during dinner, I decided to question Mrs Hoppey on the subject. After all, she seemed to know everything about the town and its inhabitants, not least from her years of digging graves. 'I have seen 'em born and I've seen 'em die, and I have even seen 'em rot to dust after death,' she would often say to me. 'There is not much that gets past the notice of old Hoppey,' and she would laugh her deep, cackling laugh that I grew to love so well.

'Mrs Hoppey, pray tell me, who was Mr Milton?' I began, digging my spoon into the mutton stew. 'Alice told me today that he was a great man who lived in Artillery Walk, but she could not really explain to me more than that.'

'Ah child, Mr Milton was a great man, of that there is no doubt,' sighed Mrs Hoppey. 'But the reasons for his greatness are manifold and complex. Each man will tell you a different story. I have heard some say that he loved the people of England and that he fought for their freedom against the tyranny of the king.'

'But surely, Mrs Hoppey, it is treason to fight against the king!' I was thinking of the colonists in America, of whom Mrs Hoppey had told me a little, who even then had declared treason against the king and were fighting against our brave army somewhere far away.

'Yes, you are right, Lizzie. But these were different times, one hundred years ago. King Charles was very different from our King

George today. He acted far less reasonably, so that some men became so enraged that they formed an army against him, and others joined the army in support of him, and the country indeed was torn apart in civil war.'

'And Mr Milton fought in the army against him?'

'I believe, Lizzie, that Mr Milton did not actually fight but he wrote pamphlets, both during and after the war.'

'Pamphlets!' I said, feeling disappointed, since thin sheets of paper and ink did not seem very valiant or heroic to me. 'How can you fight with pamphlets?'

'It is surprising what the written word can do,' said Mrs Hoppey. 'So just you persevere at school. I know how little you have learnt of reading' – and she sighed – 'but there are all sorts of worlds you can master if once you have learned that skill.' And she looked over the room to her four books – the Bible, *Pilgrim's Progress*, *Robinson Crusoe* and *Moll Flanders* – with pride.

'So what do other men say about Mr Milton?' Mrs Hoppey was inclined to go off into many digressions and I needed to remind her of the main point of our discussion.

'They say that he was mistaken in the middle of his life and led astray by misguided zeal when he was working for Oliver Cromwell. You know, Lizzie' – says she – 'that Oliver Cromwell cut off King Charles' head and ruled himself instead for some ten years. Well, our Mr Milton wrote a pamphlet as justifies the beheading of the King.'

'Surely not!' I gasped. And this man was the greatest man in Cripplegate!

'But I know very little about these matters,' continued Mrs Hoppey. 'You need to talk to Mr Poole, the old watch-maker, down in Jacob's Passage. He knows many a tale about Milton and pamphlets and Oliver Cromwell. Why, his own grandfather fought with the Roundheads, although Poole keeps quite quiet about that these days. All I know is that men say that after King Charles II returned to rule, Mr Milton went into hiding (indeed I know those who say he was hiding in Jacob's Passage with the Pooles), and then he moved to Jewin Street and wrote his great long epic poem, called *Paradise Lost*, and that is why he is really called great.'

She stopped to pause for breath at this point, and to cough with the exertion of the tale. I ran to the dresser to fetch her some gin to ease her cough, and waited several minutes while she composed herself.

'But what do *you* think, Mrs Hoppey? Why do you think he is the greatest man in Cripplegate?' I considered Mrs Hoppey to be the wisest person I knew at that time, and so I was anxious to know what was the right thing to believe.

'All I know is that he loved this parish and that he was a great Londoner,' says Mrs Hoppey. 'Why, he lived almost all his life here among us! Born in Bread Street, brought his young bride back to Aldersgate Street from Oxford, set up a school for a time in the Barbican and died in Artillery Walk. You know he was buried in our church. Nobody knows exactly where, but that's what they say.'

This was the first time I discovered the mystery about Milton's burial, but of that you have already heard a great deal, so I will not dwell on that now. But suffice it to say that I questioned Mrs Hoppey most fully on this topic, since the church and graves were topmost of our concerns.

'But most of all,' said Mrs Hoppey, after our long discussion of Milton's burial, 'I admire his courage and strength of character. For the second half of his life, he was without the use of his sight, and for the last twenty years he was completely blind. I have heard men tell how their grandfathers recall seeing Mr Milton sitting in the sun outside his house in Artillery Walk, letting the beams warm his face while yet they could never penetrate his eyes. They say he could be seen walking with a stick, accompanied by one of his daughters, going down Fore Street and men would come up to greet him and touch his arm because they had read his poem.'

'But how could he write if he could not see?' I asked. The task seemed impossible, like expecting a musical composer to write songs who could not hear or a chef to cook who could not taste. Why, I could not manage to read or write properly and I had full use of my sight!

'Ah, he would recite the lines and others would write them down. He had three daughters whom he had trained in the skill of transcription and they would record what he dictated. They were ungrateful, mind you' – says Mrs Hoppey – 'always complaining and saying that he did not treat them well. Eventually he threw them out and just lived with his new wife (his third, the other two having died). By then, he had gathered a group of young men who were all too willing to assist him with transcription, so he no longer needed his daughters in any case.'

I felt a pang with this last remark, and made a private determination never to be ungrateful or give Mrs Hoppey cause to throw me out. Always make yourself useful, Lizzie, I thought. And never become so complacent as not to realise that your skills can be replaced without too much difficulty if you do not retain your ease of temper.

'But in any event,' Mrs Hoppey was continuing, 'being a great writer is not only a matter of putting words upon a page. Mr Milton did not actually have to write in order to be called a writer.' (The notion was so paradoxical to me that I remember this last comment most particularly.) 'Mr Milton had a vision, even though he could not see. He could picture scenes in his head, he could create characters and landscapes and stories in his fancy, even though he could not hope to see them again in the world. That is what makes him great, his capacity for vision.'

'What were those visions of?' I asked.

'For that you must ask some other person. For I have not read his poem myself. I speak only from what I have heard men tell, but the language of Mr Milton is too difficult for me. I prefer Mr Defoe.' And she smiled, for he was another great Londoner and buried in Bunhill Fields with Alice's father. 'Now come along, Lizzie, that is quite enough questions for one night. For it is late, and we both must rise early in the morning.'

This was the first time I realised that Mrs Hoppey had some limits to her infinite capacity and that there were some things she did not know or could not do. I was surprised, as I knew her reading skills far exceeded my own and those of Alice at that time, but I understood now that I must speak sometime to a person who could read Milton's language and could tell me more of his divine vision.

*

It was some weeks following this conversation that I saw Mr Poole. I was in the churchyard, standing beside a half-dug grave and resting on my shovel – Mrs Hoppey had returned to the house for a short while to attend to some matter – when I saw a small, stooped, short-sighted man peering over the churchyard wall. Maybe he was hunting for his own promised plot amongst the graves or maybe he was looking for somebody, but evidently he was having the utmost difficulty seeing anything because when he detected a figure digging a grave, he assumed that I was Mrs Hoppey and hailed me as such, even though I was still several inches shorter than she at this time (Mr Poole had lost much of his sight after a lifetime of examining the tiny mechanisms of watches, as he told me later). I corrected his misapprehension and asked if I could be of assistance, but when I heard his name, I realised that this was the man whom Mrs Hoppey had mentioned who knew about Mr Milton's pamphlets.

'Mr Poole, sir, Mrs Hoppey said that I might ask you about Mr Milton.' I knew that the question seemed strange, coming from no prior conversation, but I was excited to be unexpectedly close to the possible solution of my confusion over the last few weeks and I did not want to lose the opportunity to pursue it further.

'Why, lass, that is a name I have not heard in a while. John Milton.'

I was a little anxious but Mr Poole was breaking into a smile and seemed pleased to be asked. 'A fine Radical he was,' said he, leaning on the wall. 'He stayed true to his beliefs, even when the king came back to the throne and he was sent to prison for what he had written.'

'He went to prison?' The more I heard about Mr Milton, the less I could understand why everyone said he was great.

'It was only for a few months, until his supporters managed to get him a pardon. But they were burning his books in public meanwhile. The hangman burned them, instead of burning him I suppose.'

'Burning books?' The story was so different from any stories I knew before, like Mrs Hoppey's favourite tales by Mr Defoe, that I could only repeat Mr Poole's words with astonishment.

'Indeed, I don't tell many men this, for fear it might get me into danger, but I have in my possession one of Milton's pamphlets,' continued Mr Poole. 'It belonged to my grandfather, and was spared from the hangman's flames. I can show it to you, if you wish.'

'Alas, sir, I cannot read.' This was the first time when I felt this lack most acutely. But Mr Poole put his hand on my shoulder and with a comforting murmur that he would tell me the contents, since he himself could scarcely read the words these days in any case, he led me up Red Cross Street towards his house.

I confess with the anticipation of seeing a pamphlet I forgot all about Mrs Hoppey and the necessity to stand beside our grave until she returned, especially after I saw inside Mr Poole's house. It was old and dark and the most untidy I had ever seen (Mr Poole's wife had died some years before and he lived alone, with a housekeeper to help him just two days each week), and on every surface there were watches or clocks or pieces of metal that I supposed were part of some mechanism for time-keeping. There was a sound of tick-tocking from every corner of the room, and sometimes a clock would chime the hour, apparently at a whim.

'Here it is,' Mr Poole came towards me, blowing the dust off a yellow-brown parchment. 'This is *Areopagitica*, one of the most important declarations of man's freedom. One of my most treasured possessions, besides my clocks.'

I looked down at it. I was just able to spell out slowly the first four words. *For the Liberty of.* But the next word was very long and not one I recognised.

'Unlicensed,' said Mr Poole. 'For the Liberty of Unlicensed Printing. Mr Milton was writing about the freedom to write what you want. No government should put you in prison because of a book you have written or burn pamphlets or try to change what you write before the book is published.'

'Do they really do that, Mr Poole?' I had never thought that anyone cared so much about writing before.

'Indeed they do. Even now, a man can be prosecuted for publishing something deemed blasphemous or radical or obscene. So men seek to avoid that danger by writing words that they think will be acceptable. This pamphlet by Milton is not something that is mentioned very frequently these days because men want to be safe and not to run the same course that Milton was advocating. I keep it hidden in my closet and only retrieve it when I wish to recall my grandfather and the old days.'

Mr Poole was getting very serious now, and my attention was starting to wander. I looked around the room at the watches. Mrs Hoppey must be becoming anxious about me, since I had been absent a long time. But I wished to ask one more question before I left.

'Why is it called Aria–? Ariot–? Areo–?' I could not remember the name.

'It is the hill in ancient Athens where men were free and able to speak out as openly as they wished,' said Mr Poole. 'Milton was very well read in Latin and Greek. He wrote half his books in Latin.'

I thanked Mr Poole most profusely – he even asked me for a kiss on his cold, leathery cheek – and ran back as swiftly as I could to Mrs

Hoppey. I thought she might be pleased that I had learned so much about the writer but in this assumption I was very wrong. I have never seen her in such a temper, standing red-faced in the doorway and shouting once I appeared.

'But Mrs Hoppey, Mr Poole showed me a paper which was all about a hill where men were free and writing books was very important,' I remonstrated.

'To go alone, without a companion, to the house of a man who lives a solitary life. What were you thinking of, Lizzie? You are no longer a child. You must think about your behaviour. You cannot visit just any house of any man quite freely. What evil, what sin might ensue!'

She sent me straight to bed without any supper, and I lay there in much confusion. On the one hand, Mr Poole had been talking to me about liberty and bravery and openness – and all these virtues were to be found in books and in reading. But on the other hand, Mrs Hoppey had chastised me for frequenting Mr Poole's house and implied that he might not be entirely virtuous, and I was still inclined to believe whatever Mrs Hoppey told me. So for the next few years, whenever I saw Mr Poole, I was careful to walk the other way and to avoid his glance, although once or twice I could not help casting my eyes back and I saw his sad face looking at me wistfully and with a puzzled air. And consequently it seemed to me that Milton and his hill was a source of dangerous temptation, a declaration of liberty that yet must remain secret and repressed.

*

I kept quiet about what Mr Poole had told me and never breathed a word to any soul, so that after I was married to Mr Grant and moved to his house in Beech Street and saw that he had many books and that one of them was by Mr Milton I did not do any knowing smiles or looks or say, 'This is the man who writes about the hill,' or, 'Every man must be free to write what he desires.' I was silent about the fact that I had seen the pamphlet or even that Alice and I had looked at his house beside Bunhill Fields, because I had listened to Mrs Hoppey and felt that somehow these thoughts were not suitable for a young woman and especially not a woman whom Mr Grant had thought worthy to become his bride. Instead I waited patiently for him to tell me about his book and meanwhile I cleaned around the shelves and dusted the pages of the Milton volume. Once or twice, I took the book off the shelf and opened it, but apart from the title – *Paradise Lost* – the words swam before my eyes and I could not begin to make sense of them.

But one evening, after a few months of marriage during which time Mr Grant had been reading the poetry of James Thomson and Thomas Gray to me at night, he declared that he wanted to read the most sublime poetry of all. 'Reach up to that shelf, Lizzie' – says he – 'and fetch me down the immortal book of Milton. I wish to have what in me is dark illumined once more.'

'What is dark in you, Mr Grant? There is nothing I can call dark in you. You are all light and kindness.'

'I speak but Mr Milton's words, Lizzie. This is how he begins his great poem.'

I placed the book in Mr Grant's hands and sat down on the low stool before him. My heart was beating fast because I was expecting him to speak about liberty and the unlicensed press, and I must not reveal that I had any knowledge of this. But instead he opened the pages and said, 'This is the opening of his great epic poem *Paradise Lost.*'

I remembered that this was the poem that Mrs Hoppey had said Milton had written after he came out of hiding and went to live in Jewin Street when he was completely blind.

'Why is it called an epic?'

'Epics are very long poems which have a certain grandeur,' said he. 'They tell of heroic deeds and battles and quests.'

'And are there such battles and quests in Mr Milton's poem?'

'Yes, but not fought by humans. These are deeds performed by God and the devil and the angels and our first ancestors.' And so to explain, Mr Grant told me the whole story of *Paradise Lost*, not reading from the book but recalling from his memory, his eyes shining as he described each scene for me. He told me how Satan rebelled against God and was hurled down from Heaven to Hell but that there he gathered the other fallen angels, who were now devils, and inspired them to revenge. He told me that meanwhile Adam and Eve were living in Paradise, worshipping God and tending his garden but that they were not allowed to touch the fruit of the Tree of Knowledge. One day, however, Eve was gardening alone and she met the Serpent (Satan in disguise) and he persuaded her to eat the fruit, although it was forbidden. When Adam saw her, he realised what had happened and he decided to eat the fruit too. So they were both sinful and God was angry and banished them from Heaven.

'Why did they eat the fruit if they knew it was forbidden?' I stopped Mr Grant's narrative. 'Why did God not prevent them if he is so powerful?'

'God gave them the freedom to choose whether they would obey or not. Eve was tempted by the Serpent's cunning words, and then Adam was tempted by his love for Eve. But after they had eaten, they saw the world in a different way and were ashamed about their nakedness and hid themselves.'

'How could they make the decision if they did not know everything?' I persisted. 'If they could only see sin after eating the fruit, how could they know what is sinful?'

'You ask too many questions, Lizzie,' says he. 'It is best if I read the poem. Then you can see the sublimity and majesty of the verse, and the great wisdom of Mr Milton.'

He began to read, about Satan being hurled headlong from Heaven to bottomless perdition and making long speeches to the other devils.

The sentences rolled on and on as if they were bottomless too and sometimes the order of the words were not how you expect them, so that it was hard to follow the sense, and there were no rhymes at all such as I thought were necessary for poetry. I could see that Mr Grant was truly stirred by what he was reading, and sometimes I devoted more of my attention to thinking about why he liked this writing and wishing that I could be as enraptured by it as he was than I did to listening carefully and trying to understand the meaning. But I did like Satan's speeches that were so strong and passionate and defiant, and I could comprehend his arguments which seemed clearer than some of the narrative. *Better to reign in Hell, than serve in Heaven,* I remember he said. *Here at least we shall be free.*

'I like that part,' I interrupted Mr Grant. 'Satan seems very heroic.'

'He might seem so, he might *seem* so, Lizzie,' replied he. 'But this is wrong. He is really deceitful and cowardly and evil. Once we have reached the end of the poem, then you will truly understand and will think differently about these things.'

I kept quiet after that, content to listen to Mr Grant's mellifluous voice taking me across Chaos and up to Heaven and down again and to wait until I was able to arrive at the same wise judgement as he had reached. Each evening for a couple of weeks, he read another book (for there are twelve books) and by the end I felt the tragedy of Adam and Eve's banishment with its full force, as they were driven out from Paradise by fiery angels with flaming swords and departed in tears with wandering steps, uncertain where to go, with too much liberty of choice and not enough mercy from God. But Mr Grant said that this was not the correct interpretation and that God was merciful and that he was not deliberately mischievous and calculating when he set a delicious fruit tree in his garden just so that Adam and Eve could be tempted to pick from it. I accepted his words, and put my admiration for Satan in the same secret corner of my memory where I still retained the information about Mr Poole's pamphlet and the argument for free speech.

I asked Mr Grant once why he called *Paradise Lost* sublime. He told me that something is sublime if it is bigger than our capacity to comprehend it. We might look at a huge mountain or a deep cave and not be able to see the mountain summit or detect the cave floor and then we would confront our own limitations and realise how small we were compared to the world or, more importantly, to God. He told me that Mr Burke – another writer he likes very much – maintained that this holy terror was beneficial for us, if we were not actually harmed by it, and so he advocated practising it and looking often at sublime landscapes and objects. Since I have never seen a mountain or a cave, and do not know what it is like not to be able to see the whole view if I wish – the tallest building I know is St Paul's Cathedral and even that you may see to the top of its large dome if you stand back in Cheapside and raise your head – I feel unable to give an opinion on this and cannot practise as Mr Burke would like. But I do think that terror might as easily make one think of the devil as of God, and that realising how small we are in the world is something that many people feel all the time and no benefits seem to come to them as a consequence.

I myself have reached the contrary opinion that it is better to be resourceful and think about the many capacities one is blessed with, rather than to tease oneself with thinking how small and helpless one is in comparison with the powerful universe. There are enough adverse forces in the world without courting them, I believe, and it is more profitable to focus on the little things and leave the great powers to take care of themselves.

Raphael's advice to Adam

Thus measuring things in Heav'n by things on earth
At thy request, and that you may'st beware
By what is past, to thee I have revealed
What might have else to human race been hid...
...Satan, he who envies now thy state,
Who now is plotting how he may seduce
Thee also from obedience...
...Listen not to his temptations, warn
Thy weaker; let it profit thee to have heard
By terrible example the reward
Of disobedience; firm they might have stood,
Yet fell; remember, and fear to transgress.

(Paradise Lost Book 6)

BOOK 6

The first I knew of the notice in the *Public Advertiser* was not through Mr Fountain's private communication, as we had agreed two nights previously, but through the unexpected announcement by Mr Grant. I was sitting Saturday mid-morning on the front step of my house, on account of the intense summer heat, shelling peas that I had just bought at the market, when Mr Grant appeared suddenly, wiping his sweating brow and clutching a crumpled paper. His arrival was most surprising, for I had thought that he was due to be working at Mr Strong's for the duration of the day, so I jumped up quite flustered, for it seemed to me there must be something seriously the matter.

'Why, Mr G, sit down, sit down, pray tell me what has happened!' I cried, and I moved my peas to one side and made a space for him on the step.

'It's the paper, we are in the paper!' sighed he, and he pushed the newspaper towards me.

'Please read it to me, my hands are full at the moment,' I replied, glad to find an excuse so readily, for I was both excited and anxious, but I did not want Mr Grant to see this. So he reached for his glasses and read the paragraph which was to mark the beginning of our publick shame and undoing.

The Public Advertiser, no. 19499. Price: Three-pence Half-penny

Saturday August 7th 1790.

MILTON. The place of interment of this celebrated Poet has been much sought after, but has hitherto remained unknown to the world:- Conjecture had, indeed, fixed it to Cripplegate Church; but supposition was, on Wednesday, converted into certainty; the workmen, who are repairing that fabrick, having dug up the coffin in which the remains of that sublime bard had been deposited, and on which is the inscription intended to identify its contents.

When he had finished reading, he took off his glasses and sat silent for a minute, looking at the dusty street in front of him.

'Fountain,' said he at last quietly, 'Fountain has let us down. He must have spoken to somebody who writes for the paper. I should have known the fellow is not to be trusted.'

I trembled a little inside at this point, for I wondered why Mr Grant felt that Mr Fountain had failed him in the past and was not to be trusted and I was uncertain what he meant by these words. So I decided to move the discussion to a different topic.

'How did you hear about this news, Mr G?' I asked.

'Mr Strong came in this morning with the newspaper,' replied he. 'He was scarlet with rage, pacing up and down the room, throwing papers around, and coming up to shake me by the shoulders more than once, as I sat at his desk. He blames me, you understand, Lizzie. He blames me for making public what was originally just a private investigation conducted by himself, Mr Cole and me. He knows I went off with Cole to Fountain's house to down a couple of ales after our discovery. Indeed I led him to believe that I had drunk so many that I could not rise from my bed the next morning. He thinks me a drunk and a dissolute, who would let slip a secret when deep in my cups. Did he but know that I myself presided over the excavation the following morning, that I watched as the men lifted up the coffin again, and did nothing when Holmes peeled back the lid and Laming pulled off the shroud and – great God, Lizzie!' He broke off suddenly here, as he remembered the full details of the scene.

'Listen, Mr G,' said I, laying my hand upon his knee and bringing him back from his reverie. 'I think there is not so very much to fear. For it seems to me, from what you read, as if the newspaper has recounted the story in considerable error. Did not you say that it is reported there is an inscription on the coffin, identifying the contents? But we saw that there was no such inscription. And does the report not say that workmen dug up the coffin and suggest that the coffin with its inscription is still unearthed to be viewed? This writer is very wide of the truth, for we know that the workmen were not present for the disinterment, and that the coffin has been buried again. It seems' – I concluded – 'that you cannot always believe everything you read in the newspapers, despite how full of authority and how widely circulated they are.'

'That is very true, Lizzie,' said my husband, stirring a little from his despondency in his love of reflecting upon matters of writing and politics and other intellectual issues. 'Here every day I have been reading about the revolution in France and the doings of the National Assembly and growing more and more apprehensive, but maybe those reports too are not always accurate. Writers working quickly may not always have time to verify their facts.'

'In any case, Mr G,' said I, bringing him back from Paris to think about the quarrel in our street, 'Mr Strong is probably only enraged because he was not the first to speak to the newspaper himself. You know well how he likes to command the affairs in the street. No doubt he thought himself to broadcast this news of his own discovery, only to find now that another writer has beaten him to the game.'

'Hush, Lizzie!' said Mr Grant. 'I know Mr Strong thinks perhaps a little too well of himself, but you have a harsh tongue.'

'Nonsense, Mr G!' says I, a little more defiant than usual on account of my secret pride at my actions over the previous few days. 'You know as well as I do that Mr Strong has been pushing himself forward as the pillar of St Giles' Church, foremost in the plans for the renovation work and always talking with the rector about the building and the school and the assistance for the poor. Why, he even talked with Mrs Hoppey last week, telling her to manage the churchyard differently, she who's been digging graves there these forty years! No' – I shook my head –'I am not being too harsh and you know it indeed. He's a headstrong, pompous man, Mr G, far inferior to you, and he probably fancied himself as the sole proprietor of Milton's memory.'

'I daresay you are right, Lizzie,' said Mr Grant, his anger subsiding now with a sigh. 'Perhaps if I return now to his house to continue his letters, he will have calmed himself, and will be comporting himself with more propriety. Indeed, I think I must return' – said he, rising to his feet – 'for there is still much work to be completed, and besides, I need to show him, if I can, that there is no real harm done and that I have done nothing of which I should be ashamed.'

'Indeed, you have not, Mr G,' said I, and I patted his arm to emphasise the point, for he looked as if he were faltering a little, perhaps recalling the second disinterment on Wednesday forenoon and the handful of hair he had grasped and placed now I knew not where. 'Of course,' I continued, 'this report might mean that visitors will flock to the church, believing that they can view the coffin with the inscription – but we should not worry, for most likely they will simply see the church full of workmen, the floor reconstituted and no casket in sight, and then they will depart again. It is of no great concern.'

And Mr Grant, mollified now by my words, agreed with me – 'Yes,' said he, 'there is nothing to see in St Giles' now, nothing of Milton besides Strong's story, and no doubt this will disappear soon too, along with the body, since there are far more important matters abroad which should occupy the public attention.'

'Yes, Mr G, indeed,' said I, trying to seem as sober and wise as he, and concerning myself with France and the Bastille and other such issues that he often spoke to me about. But all the time, my mind was turning over and over the implications of this news report and what it meant for Mr Fountain and me. For if visitors would come to St Giles', after reading the paper, and find that there was nothing to be seen, then surely they would hide their disappointment by calling into Fountain's tavern and soon they would hear there about our parcels of hair and bones and riches would inevitably follow! Our plan – my plan that I had hatched but two days before – seemed to be working. The market for Milton was set fair!

*

It was that very same day that Mr Neve first came to Cripplegate. He was among the earliest of our outside visitors and the most fateful, although I did not encounter him on his first visit. Young Hawkesworth broke the news to me that afternoon, Hawkesworth who had tried to buy his way in to see Milton with kisses but three days before. Ever the bold rascal, he hailed me from some way down the street as I was returning from the meat market, bearing a fine piece of mutton for the weekend. He was standing at the corner of Fore Street and White Cross Street, a motley crowd of youths gathered around him whom he was entertaining with quips and tales of his misadventures. He was always telling whoever would listen to him of his latest conquests of the Cripplegate and Whitechapel girls, and it must be said that he is a handsome fellow, though he is scarcely more than a stripling, tall and fair, with chest and arms already broad from hard coffin-making for Mr Ascough. But I took exception to his presumption and his juvenile vanity, and so I was always ready to remind him of his age and the distance between us. So now, as I walked along Fore Street, he broke off from the group, who were still laughing loudly at something he had said, and came quickly over to me, pushing back his hair so as to draw attention to himself as he did so.

'Well, Lizzie, love, it seems Cripplegate has achieved fame, and it is all due to us!' declared he, daring to put an arm around my waist and whirling me about.

'I don't understand your meaning, Thomas,' said I formally, slipping from his grasp and standing at a distance. He is always so forward, and I resented this deeply, I a married woman of five-and-twenty!

'Have not you heard?' replied he. 'It's the talk of the street here. Some gentleman from Holborn – one of the inns he said – has been here inquiring about Milton's body, since he read about it in the *Public Advertiser*, and I sold him one of the poet's teeth and a piece of the coffin for two shillings.' And he reached into his pocket, and pulled out two shilling coins wrapped in an old dirty kerchief, which he held out to me proudly as proof of his tale.

'Thomas, tell me what happened, I must know, it is very important,' said I urgently, pulling him by the arm now towards the churchyard, so that we might talk privately. I think he might have got the wrong idea of what I intended by this, saucy fellow that he is, but I was not concerned, so anxious was I to hear of this gentleman and of his unusual transaction with Hawkesworth. Two shillings for a tooth and a bit of rusty lead!

We sat down upon the bench – the bench indeed where so many important conversations had taken place in my life – and I pressed Hawkesworth to tell me everything that had occurred that day. He told me, of course, that Mr Neve had come to St Giles' having read the report in the *Advertiser*, wanting to see the coffin, but was disappointed when there was nothing to be viewed, but that he had noticed Hawkesworth near the entrance to the church and inquired of him what further he could tell him of the story. Then Hawkesworth had told the tale, embellishing, it must be said, his part in the proceedings and omitting – I was privately relieved – everything of Mr Grant's part in it, and hardly anything of mine. 'So' – he finished – 'thinking that Mr Neve (for that of course was the gentleman's name) might want some visible proof of our find, I showed him the reliques I had taken when you guided me to the coffin on Wednesday, Lizzie, and he immediately offered to buy them from me. I had not thought previously that there might be a value in them nor had I intended to sell them at all. But I calculated quick as anything and asked the largest amount I dare, and he paid it up front, there upon the spot. I was confounded, I confess, Lizzie–' (and I smiled at this unusual admission of weakness from him) 'for I never thought a bit of tooth and a scrap of old metal could be worth so much to anyone.'

'Never mind his foolishness,' said I. I confess that I used that word, for I did so deliberately to set in motion the belief on the streets that these reliques were not worth very much and only a fool would pay for them, since I did not want other people to take the fancy of selling their remains and so compete with Fountain for our market. I was learning already, you can see, from my mistake three days before. So I continued with Hawkesworth, 'Tell me, however. Did this gentleman say anything else?'

'Yes' – replied he – 'he pressed me with so many questions about the story and the other men present at the disinterment, and where it was possible to buy other reliques, and whether those sellers were at home today. I took him, in fact, to Mr Laming in Red Cross Street, since I knew that he had taken some bone and hair – for he has been talking of little else to anyone who might be willing to listen in the subsequent days – and I thought that he, of all the people present at the disinterment, might be willing to part with them if money were to be offered in exchange. But old Laming was from home, so this gentleman said that he would return on Monday.'

97

I could not forbear from asking Hawkesworth why he did not take the gentleman to Mr Fountain, but he simply winked at me (I fear he knows more than he should about my former life before I was married) and said that he had not been at leisure to do so, for he had had a commitment to Mr Ascough which he could not postpone any longer.

'Well, I thank you for telling me this, Hawkesworth,' said I, eventually, rising to my feet and gathering my bags together. 'It seems as if fame indeed is coming to Cripplegate. But pray, can you do one thing for me?'

'What is that Lizzie?' said he, moving one step closer.

'I wish' – said I – 'when this gentleman returns on Monday, that you will not mention to him that it was I who let the people in to the church on Wednesday and took sixpence from each to shew them the body, and especially' – says I – 'I do not wish him to know that I allowed people to break pieces off the body. Not that there is any great harm in that,' added I quickly, 'for it is a mere corpse after all.' ('I've seen plenty of them,' says Hawkesworth. 'And so have I,' quipped I in return, not one to be outdone.) 'No,' said I seriously again, 'but I do not wish Mr Grant to know more about last Wednesday than he needs to know. He is of a sensitive and delicate nature, and such things might trouble him.'

'I understand, Lizzie,' whispers Hawkesworth, 'but what's it worth to me?'

'You saucy lad,' I grinned, but I let him press his lips to mine and push his hand down into my bosom hurriedly, all for the sake of my marriage and the respect which Mr Grant had for me and my desire not to lose it.

'You have my word, Lizzie,' smiled Hawkesworth eventually, 'and the finest breasts in Cripplegate to boot!' And he jumped over the stones to the street, before I could chastise him.

*

The following day was Sunday, and we attended the morning service at St Giles' as usual. We sit always in a pew about halfway down the church, behind Mr Strong and Mr Cole and of course behind Mr Whitbread, who lives in the big Drewry House in Beech Street, but in front of Ascough and Laming and the Draper widows from the almshouses at the back. When I worked for Mrs Hoppey, I sat with her over on the other side of the church, further from the front, but Mr Grant, although he is wise and compassionate, still believes that it is important for the good order of the country that everyone keeps his position from year to year. That way – he says – according to his favourite writer, Mr Burke, the social fabrick is maintained, and, since I spent some time embroidering a cushion for our pew and every Sunday during the sermon I look at the stitching with pride, I am inclined to agree with him. So on this Sunday, I sat in our pew and nodded across the aisle to Mrs Lackington, the bookseller's wife, who was with child again, and smiled politely as Mr Strong and his wife and children walked past us on their way to their position at the front. There were a couple of ladders right at the back of the church, but in other respects there was no sign of the excavation work and disinterment which had occurred but four days before. I looked most particularly around the area of the common-council-men's-pew at the end of the service, when we were free to walk about and admire other women's bonnets, but the stones were all neatly laid back again and some of the council men had been sitting there, as if nothing had happened.

I was secretly gripped by an urgent desire to find out whether Mr Fountain had sold any more of our parcels in the last day, since the *Advertiser* report was out, and whether he had heard anything about the gentleman who had questioned Hawkesworth. I had seen nothing of Fountain since our passionate meeting on Thursday evening. There had scarcely been an opportunity and besides, despite the fact that

I kept recalling our embrace by the beer barrels with sharp pleasure, I was also aware that the liaison was fraught with guilt and danger especially where Mr Grant was concerned. There was no chance of meeting Fountain in church – he never attends on a Sunday morning, owing, so he says, to the tavern being so busy on a Saturday night and the task of clearing up on a Sunday morning – but I kept speculating on the possibility that we might run into him in Beech Street in the normal course of events, and I might, by some signal, ascertain what was the state of our joint venture. On the other hand, while I knew we would not meet Fountain in church, I was a little concerned that we might encounter the other fellows now participating in the market – Haslib, Ascough, Laming, Hawkesworth or Holmes – and that they might let slip, in front of Mr Grant, some mention of the sixpence payment to me, or jokes about rival sales of teeth or jawbones, or some other such sally. Indeed, I had just noticed William Haslib at the back of the church, deep in conversation with Mr Ascough, and glancing occasionally – I thought – in my direction, when Mrs Hoppey came bustling up to me.

'Why how do ye do, Lizzie!' says she, as warm as ever and with a ready embrace. 'And how is Mr Grant today?'

'I am weary indeed, Mrs Hoppey,' says my husband, coming swiftly to my side. 'Mr Strong has kept me at the desk these three days past until well after eight in the evening, copying and writing, until I swear my eyes are weakened well nigh to bleariness. It was all I could do to stumble back dazed along Beech Street in an evening, like blind old Milton himself.'

They both laughed, and Mrs Hoppey looked at me and said, 'Lizzie will take care of you, when you return home, of that I am sure!' And I flushed with pleasure, for I love to hear Mrs Hoppey's faith and pride in me, after all these years.

'And how do ye do, Mrs Hoppey?' I asked her in return.

'In truth' – said she – 'I am almost as weary and anxious as Mr Grant.

I have had three burials already this week, and now I have just been told that a mother has been struck down in childbirth in Grub Street, and I must have the grave dug by noon tomorrow, and I cannot tell how I will complete this, for I must attend a meeting with Ascough tomorrow forenoon, to discuss the supply of coffins, and the house needs attention, and my gout is playing up again moreover and–' At this point she was overwhelmed with the thought of all the tasks which awaited her, and Mr Grant and I helped her to a pew.

I came to a quick decision. 'I will help you, Mrs Hoppey' – says I – 'I can assist in the house this afternoon, and then tomorrow morning I will dig the grave while you are with Mr Ascough. It has been a few years since I last dug a grave, but I daresay that I will discover my skills again.'

Mrs Hoppey seized my hand in gratitude, her eyes sparkling with love as ever. 'I thank ye, Lizzie,' says she. 'I will be calm now that I know that the burial is taken care of. You are both such good people, my dear,' and she looked up to Mr Grant now too with a smile, for I think she considers him almost as a son too, especially following the time when she cared for him when his first wife was sick. 'Will you indulge my fancy, and come back to my house now for some cheese and ale? I have a little fish too, which I bought yesterday,' she added, looking extra happy at the thought.

So Mr Grant and I accompanied Mrs Hoppey back to her house, for a simple but cheerful repast, where we talked of the old days when I was her servant and I dug graves and polished the hearth until Mr Grant came to rescue me – we joked in this fashion! – and Mrs Hoppey became quite merry with the ale, and after lunch she retired to her bed for a noisy sleep, while I resumed my old position at the table, polishing her pots and kneading the fresh bread for the morrow. So with all this conversation and work, there was no time to think even about Milton and Mr Fountain and what the latest word about the disinterment was on the street. Mr Grant, it seemed, continued to be ignorant of the affair, and I was content to let matters take their course.

*

The following day I was up bright and early to dig the grave for Mrs Hoppey, before the burial at midday. The weather was hotter than ever, the sun scorching down from a cloudless blue sky by eight o'clock in the morning, and I could smell the stench of the Fore Street drain hanging thick in the air before I even reached St Giles'. I was anxious to get the majority of the digging completed before the sun got much higher in the sky, and so I set to work with alacrity, only stopping occasionally to swig from a bottle of ale I had brought with me for the purpose. The earth was baked hard – we had had no rain for more than two weeks so far as I can recall – and I had to swing the pickaxe with all the skill I had acquired over many years to make any impression at all. As I was taking a break, sitting on a neighbouring tombstone and wiping my brow with my favourite kerchief, I noticed Hawkesworth passing the gate, with an unknown gentleman. I knew he was a gentleman, for he wore a spotless jacket and waistcoat of the finest cotton, and a pair of costly spectacles upon his nose. He caught my eye, and I could tell that he was curious and made as if to enter the graveyard in order to make my acquaintance. But Hawkesworth took his arm and propelled him further up Fore Street (presumably, I know now, on his way to Mr Laming) and so the gentleman complied. I guessed the identity of the gentleman, and was silently grateful for Hawkesworth's self-restraint on this occasion. Clearly my kiss had had some effect.

I know now, of course, that Mr Neve was making strenuous enquiries of many of the participants in the disinterment, to develop a complete narrative of what had taken place that fateful August morning, and that as part of these enquiries he was meeting those men who had taken reliques and he was making purchase of them, purely to be able to restore them later to Milton's grave. But at the time, I knew only that a highly-educated gentleman was being guided around the streets by Hawkesworth, wanting to buy all the remains that were available, and I was trembling with anxiety inside lest he make himself known to Mr Fountain. On the one hand, I was concerned that Mr Fountain might tell him the whole story of what had happened and about my donation to him of the jawbone and the parcels of remains for sale. But on the other hand, I was also hoping, secretly, that he would somehow purchase one of our elegant packages, at a high price, without asking too many questions. So as I dug deeper and deeper into the hard, clay soil, my mind flapped this way and that, as changeable as a gladsome flag blowing gaily in the wind at Bartholomew's fair.

When Mr Grant returned home from work that evening, he appeared even more lost in thought than usual. He sat at the table, a cup of tea untouched before him, and his eyes focused somewhere beyond the open doorway, where the last of the barrow men were packing up their goods and the sweepers were clearing away the rotting vegetables which had fallen there during the day.

'Lizzie,' said he at last, turning round to look at me for the first time where I stood stirring the evening stew, 'I am at a loss what to think. The talk of the Milton disinterment just will not go away, despite my best efforts to avoid it, but what it means for all of us I cannot tell.'

'What has happened now, Mr G?' I asked, as innocent as a newborn kid.

'Some gentleman from Furnival's Inn has been busy making inquiries all day, following that atrocious *Advertiser* report,' he replied. 'He came knocking for Mr Strong this morning, and I let him in a little warily, I can tell you. I thought, given Mr Strong's anger on Saturday, that he would send him packing, soon as look on him. But, no. He was closeted with Strong for more than two hours in the front parlour, talking and talking, and afterwards Mr Strong came out, all puffed and proud with the excitement. "Grant", says he to me, "we have done

103

a great thing. This gentleman – his name is a Mr Philip Neve – is a renowned scholar of Milton. He tells me that we discovered the body of the greatest poet this nation has produced, a sincere and fervent lover of his country who sought freedom with a resolution undeterred by whatever trials and obstacles came his way". (Of course, I knew all this very well, Mrs G, but Mr Strong appears to have been unfamiliar with the details of Milton's life.) "We now share his glory" – continued he – "as the men who were able to bring back his memory once again at a time when, with all this shocking upheaval in France, our nation needs him most. Indeed, my name of Strong – and I suppose your name too, Grant – will be forever linked with that of the illustrious John Milton". And you know, Lizzie, he even put his arm around my shoulders, and suggested that we should drink a toast to Milton and to our fortunes, now forever connected with the Bard. He brought out an old brandy, even though it was still early in the afternoon, and he poured us both a large glass, so large in fact that I might have felt quite sleepy all the afternoon, if I had not been troubled by one painful concern.'

'Pray, what is that, husband?' I asked him, sitting down now at the table beside him.

'Well, all that time' – he continued – 'while Mr Strong was talking about how he had described the coffin to Mr Neve and how he was able to guess the probable size and dimensions of the body from the measurement of the coffin, I could not forbear recalling privately that we had returned the following morning and looked at the very body inside. Far from measuring the casket, we had peeled back the lid and gazed upon the head and chest and' – he broke off now for a few seconds, overcome with the horror of the memory – 'did not I even take a handful of the hair?' And he ran his fingers through his own few sprouts of hair in frenzy now, as pictures of the event came flooding back upon his fancy. 'I reached in' – persisted he – 'and felt that cold, damp mane of hair, and I was overwhelmed with the excitement of touching the visible mark of that man's genius – his thick flowing locks – and so I just pulled slightly and it came away in my hand and – O Lizzie, why did I so?'

Mr Grant continued to groan and rub his head in an agony of remorse for quite some time. 'Why did I not show restraint?' he kept repeating to himself. 'What moved me to act so licentiously? *Licence they mean, when they cry liberty* – that's what the wise bard wrote.' At length, however, he sat up and looked at me with more purpose. 'I am resolved, Lizzie' – said he – 'to find this Mr Neve and give him the hair which I took from the body. Maybe he can find some more worthy use for it. Or maybe it could even be restored to the grave. I know the gentleman lives in Holborn. It is probable that I can make inquiries of people living in the parish and locate his dwelling.' And he started to his feet, as if he were planning to walk to the west end of town that very minute with the locks in his hand.

'Wait, Mr G, I have another idea!' cried I, hurriedly. 'Sit down and I will tell you.' I quickly gathered my thoughts and argued thus. 'We do not know this Mr Neve. We do not know what manner of man he may be nor what he plans to do with this information. It may be that he wishes to laud us all for revealing the glory of Milton. It may be, on the other hand, that he wishes to use this information for his own ends in some way, to add to his reputation or even' – and here I stopped briefly, for the idea had only just struck me – 'because he wishes to find the exact location of the grave so that he can effect a disinterment of his own. It is best to wait a little before you approach him, so that we can determine how this stranger will make publick the account of what has happened. Besides' – here I whispered, even though we sat in our own house, for the thought was a little shameful, even to me – 'it is likely that he knows nothing of you taking the hair, and nobody else will tell him, without having to reveal their own share in the event. Best, then, not to mention it, and perhaps it will be soon forgotten. Where have you put the hair, husband?'

'In my box of important papers, beside my will and the last letter from Mangan,' replied he hesitantly.

'That sounds safe enough' – says I – 'and that is where it should stay for the time being. We must remain cautious during these times, Mr G, and do nothing precipitate.'

'I am a little reluctant' – said he with a sigh – 'but I will be guided by you on this occasion, Lizzie. After all, you were wiser than me last week, and hung back when all the rest of us were reaching in and violating the body – Great God, why did we so! It makes my blood boil now, to think of it. Only you showed judicious restraint, and indeed you devoted the rest of the day to preventing others from violent intrusion and sacrilege. We should all have learned from you, my dear!' And he kissed me tenderly then, his worries subsiding under the strength of his affection for me.

He tucked in then to his stew, his fury abated, even if – I suppose – he occasionally thought of the hair coiled up beside his documents with a pang of guilty concern. But can you imagine my feelings at this moment? There I was, held up as a paragon of virtue and wisdom by my much older husband, because I had not touched the body, and had indeed protected it from being further violated. It was my perfection and restraint that were acting as an example and inspiration to him, in his hour of confusion and self-recrimination. But all the while, I was in fact the chief architect behind a violation, the extent of which he was still happily ignorant. It was at my instigation that Fountain had obtained the jawbone, it was under my watch that half of Cripplegate had broken off pieces of the body and coffin, and it was prompted by my fancy that the market for the remains had widened from simply our street to possibly the whole of London.

Of course I could not disabuse Mr Grant of his illusion about me, when it allowed him tranquilly to fall asleep that night. And in fact, I thought that perhaps the truth about my actions would never come to light, that Mr Neve would not discover or reveal the details about the aftermath of the disinterment and my participation in it. But I confess, that this evening marked the beginning of the change in my feelings about the event, from excitement and pride to uneasy guilt and anxiety, now that I knew so clearly Mr Grant's opinion on the matter.

The midway point.

Half yet remains unsung, but narrower bound
Within the visible diurnal sphere;
Standing on earth, nor rapt above the pole,
More safe I sing with mortal voice, unchanged
To hoarse or mute, though fall'n on evil days,
On evil days though fall'n, and evil tongues;
In darkness, and with dangers compassed round,
And solitude...

(Paradise Lost Book 7)

BOOK 7

That night, I had the first of my disturbing dreams that have troubled my sleep in the months since. I took some time to fall asleep, and lay awake fitfully long after I could hear Mr Grant's methodical and relentless snoring. But eventually I must have drifted away because I remember vividly that I seemed to be running down Beech Street with the clump of Milton's hair in my hand. At some points in the dream, I was also holding the vegetables that I had bought for Mrs Hoppey, and I was thirteen years old again and dancing and skipping with Alice. But just as I was about to give over what was in my hand, I looked down and the green stalks had changed to yellow-brown, damp, stinking strands. Suddenly Mr Grant was also present sitting beside me, with his book, and we were reading *Paradise Lost* together. The words blurred and swam before my eyes, and I knew, since I could not read them, that I would need to recite the poem from memory, which, as I scarcely understand it, is almost impossible. But somehow in my dream, though I knew neither the words nor the sense, somehow each line seemed to come of its own accord. I was reciting Milton and Mr Grant was looking at me proudly and nodding and sometimes joining in himself. I was growing in confidence and almost enjoying the process and the achievement of impressing him. But then suddenly my facility seemed to fail me, the words stopped coming to my lips, and I could not fathom how to avoid the inevitable exposure and shame, even while at my bosom I became aware more and more of the hard press of an awkward bone tucked inside my dress.

The humiliation and embarrassment of this potential crisis seemed to be coming ever closer until with a start I awoke and found that the book, which Mr Grant had been reading before going to sleep, had been dropped in the bed between us and its corner was now jutting into my breast most uncomfortably. He was still in quiet slumber, now scarcely making a sound besides his gentle breathing in and out, and I lay and watched him to calm my anxiety after the dream. What a foolish dream, Lizzie, I thought to myself. Here is your husband who actually held the clump of hair and he is dozing peacefully. Try to stay as brave and strong as always, and all will be well. After all, soon you may also be rich with the profits of the sales and will be able to buy nice trinkets and forget about the present doubts.

*

During the last few days, however, I had received no word from Mr Fountain. He had said nothing about our joint venture nor if he had talked with Mr Neve nor what had been the consequence of the *Advertiser* report. No word, indeed, for five days, not since the previous Thursday when we had made the pact, and I was growing very curious and by Tuesday morning, I confess, not a little uneasy. Was he well? Had he been taken unexpectedly from home? Had the store of parcels somehow been raided? Or was the market so furious he had had no time to come and tell me the latest news? Anxious questions such as these fluttered at my breast until I decided, waking late after my troubled sleep and disturbed night, that I would venture along to the tavern to make inquiries after I had completed my morning tasks. My walk back from the market in Jewin Street would take me past Fountain's house, after all, and what was the harm in stopping by to discuss matters with him, having a quiet laugh together – I was determined not to repeat the passionate temptation of Thursday night – and setting my mind at ease, well before I was expected to attend to my husband again?

The sun was already high in the sky when I set off for the market, and I discovered once I arrived that most of the women I knew had already made their necessary purchases for the day. There was only a small amount of milk at the bottom of the churn that was tapped for me and when I reached the stall for meat I discovered that there were only a few pieces of mutton left and that a small crowd of women had gathered around the seller, jostling with each other to be served first and shouting louder and louder in frustration. The man selling the meat – a young lad who was helping his father for the day – was trying unsuccessfully to pacify the women and to encourage them to form a line, but I think his youth counted against him for nobody paid him any attention. I myself was annoyed that I had failed to arrive at the market earlier and was determined to make amends by forcing my way to the front of the line, late as I was, so I surged forward and began using my elbows as vigorously and expertly as the next woman.

My efforts produced the inevitable outcry from the other women and some well-aimed shoves and pinches from the more aggressive members of the group, and it seemed as if, despite my years of practice in fending off rivals at the market, I would have to acknowledge defeat and retreat to the quieter vegetable stall. But then the small, thin woman standing at the front of the crowd turned her head and I recognised that it was Sarah Newton, the daughter of Mr Laming, the pawnbroker. She noticed me at the same time, because I was at the centre of the disturbance, and she called to me that she could purchase some meat for me too if I liked. Some of the other women protested at this, because it meant that there might be less mutton remaining for them and I was not meekly waiting my turn like the rest, but Sarah ignored them and stood her ground beside the stall more solidly and determinedly than before.

'Why, I thank you, Sarah,' said I gladly, when she freed herself from the crowd and gave me the precious parcel of mutton. 'I usually arrive at the market much earlier than this, but I was delayed this morning (I did not want to confess to her about my bad dream). You saved me from offering Mr Grant nothing but potatoes and gruel for dinner!'

'I am never usually so late at market either, Lizzie,' said she. 'But I was compelled to spend some time opening the shop myself this morning. My father seemed to be distracted today, most unlike his usual self, more interested in reading a book than in laying out his clocks and baubles for sale.'

'A book!' I echoed. 'And to think that he almost missed having meat for dinner because he was reading a book.'

'O Lizzie, that is the least of my concerns. My father has been in strange spirits for the last week. At times he is more animated than I have seen him in years, dancing around the shop and re-arranging all the shelves and counting his money. But at other times, like this morning for instance, he has scarcely noticed me at all, or indeed anything around him – especially his obligations to the shop – but he is only interested in reading.'

By this stage we were walking together up Red Cross Street, our morning's shopping being complete, and Sarah Newton had pushed her arm through mine as she confided her anxieties. As we drew near Laming's house, she suggested I came in to see how he did, I think in the hope that I might rouse him from his distraction. I have always liked old Mr Laming, since the days when he used to come and drink an ale with Mrs Hoppey after church on Sundays. He would entertain us with his tales of the shop, and tell a few jokes and tickle me under the chin when I was young, and he always seemed in good cheer and full of energy and ideas for business. Besides I felt in his daughter's debt this morning, after she had helped me at the meat stall, so I decided to call in despite the fact that this would mean that I would reach Fountain's house later than I had intended. Besides I was curious to see for myself Mr Laming's mood and strange alteration in character, not least since I had not had a chance to speak to him since our activities following the disinterment the previous week.

I should explain at this point that Mr Laming lived with his daughter and her family in Red Cross Street, his wife having sadly died a few years before. His wife's death, however, had not dented his zeal for his business, and he was usually always to be seen in the front room of the house, either laying out the watches and necklaces and even old shoes which people had brought him in return for a loan, or leaning over the counter and deep in negotiation with some poor, needy journeyman or a harassed and anxious couple. Men will often cavil at the pawnbroking trade, accusing its agents of being extortionists and cunning foxes, preying on the desperation and naivety of the poor and needy, and I dare say that there are many such men, who will take a valuable jewel from an innocent man in exchange for a loan which is a fraction of its worth, or they will charge impossible rates of interest so that their victims can never hope to redeem their possessions and they sink further and further into debt and dependency. But Mr Laming was not like these men. I have never needed to resort to a pawnbroker, because I have been fortunate and also am careful with my money, working out the calculations of credit and debit each month. But if I did, for some reason, need a loan suddenly, I would have had no hesitation in seeking help from Mr Laming. For he would give money to his clients, in exchange for their possessions, because he could see that they were in want and desired to assist. Of course, he was serious in his business and calculated carefully the value of each object – do not mistake me. He would expect men to pay more than the value of the original loan if they wanted to redeem their possessions, and if those objects were not claimed within the year, he would sell them, as any other pawnbroker would do. But Mr Laming was fair and reasonable, and he would listen sympathetically to the tale of each customer, judging whether in this case they were able to produce the money soon and so he could wait another month or two before he closed the deal.

Today, however, there were no customers in the shop and Mr Laming was sitting behind the counter, on a high stool, rubbing his bald pate absent-mindedly (he had neglected to wear his customary wig) and balancing a large, yellowing and dusty book upon his knees. He was carefully moving his finger across the line of words on the page and whispering softly to himself, his spectacles slipped to the end of his thin beak of a nose.

'What are you reading there, Mr Laming?' I asked quietly after a few minutes of silence when it was apparent that he was oblivious to my arrival.

He jumped up from his stool with surprise, dropping his book to the floor with a thud, and held on to the counter to steady himself. It seemed to be taking him some time to recognise me, as he had been lost in perusing the volume, so I asked my question again.

'I am reading *Paradise Lost*, the great epic poem by Mr Milton, Lizzie, my dear,' said he (he has always treated me almost as another daughter). 'I confess that I had never read anything by Milton before, but after our discovery of the body last week and my acquiring – well you know what we came away with that day, Lizzie.' At this point I swear that Mr Laming, the greatest pawnbroker in Cripplegate, blushed at the memory of the previous week and looked a little confused.

'What did you take, Mr Laming? There was so much commotion and excitement that day that I cannot be sure what you acquired?' All I could recall – and it came to me as a sudden flash before my eyes – was Mr Laming waving a leg bone in the air, but I had thought he had thrown it back into the coffin.

But Mr Laming was bending down to pick up his book again and set his stool upright that had been knocked by his sudden movement.

I was certain that he had heard me but was choosing not to reply, so I pressed again with my questions.

'Have you met with the gentleman from Furnival's Inn? I know that he has visited Cripplegate twice to make inquiries from those who were present at Milton's disinterment. Young Hawkesworth was shewing him around.'

Mr Laming grunted crossly. 'Yes, I met with him. Mr Neve.'

I was surprised at Mr Laming's terseness. Normally he was most fulsome in his conversation, always full of stories to tell, as he leant over his counter, of his long years of experience and the customers he had met. He could regale me with the sorrows and tribulations to which a lifetime of helping those in great financial distress had exposed him. But today it seemed he was only half aware of my presence and irritated by my interruptions upon his thoughts.

'What did Mr Neve want?' I persisted. 'Did he ask about what you acquired of Milton? Did you have anything to sell him?' In truth, I wanted to know if Mr Fountain and I had competition for our parcels in the coming days.

'Sell? Sell!' barked Mr Laming. I had never seen him so out of temper. Normally he is such a genial man, always with a smile and a kind gleam in his eye. 'I have a few reliques, a few reliques I acknowledge. But God forbid that I would be persuaded to sell them!'

I looked around me at the shop, where all the poor treasures of the neediest families of Cripplegate were stored, the clocks and shoes that were scarcely of use to anyone but which Mr Laming had carefully calculated for their value and was keeping in return for a few coins. It had seemed to me that he, more than any of us, would be eager to make a profit out of the remains of Milton and with more opportunity and experience to do so. But clearly I had somehow offended him.

He was looking at his book again and I was relieved to see that his mood was softening and he was caught up in excitement once again.

'Adam's dream,' he was saying, his voice going low with wonder as he began to pace around the room. 'I have just been reading it this morning. Adam was asleep and awake at the same time. While he slept in Paradise, God took one of his ribs from his body and formed a woman, Eve, out of the bone, with the *cordial spirits warm* still. Adam's *cell of Fancy* was left open and he watched the process even while he drowsed. What a miracle, Lizzie! What a marvel! Why here Milton writes (and he pulled me towards the book which he was jabbing with his bony finger) that "the rib he formed and fashioned with his hands; under his forming hands a creature grew". Just think about the power of creation, all that from a bone!'

But then Mr Laming stopped suddenly, clutching his book and looking at me aghast.

'But then the dream disappeared,' he whispered. 'The wonder cannot always remain. See, here.' He pointed to some lines in the book again, which of course I could not read, but he proceeded to intone anyway.

'"She disappeared, and left me dark, I waked
To find her, or for ever to deplore
Her loss, and other pleasures all abjure".

The dream comes and goes, Lizzie. It ebbs and flows, it comes and goes.'

He stood frozen to the spot, like one of his ticking clocks that has been neglected and whose hands slow down until they rest upon some unlikely number. But I touched his arm to rouse him from his melancholy reverie and led him back to his stool.

'Do not agitate yourself so much, Mr Laming. It is only an old tale,' said I. 'In any case, I know that Eve did not disappear but lived happily with Adam in Paradise until they ate the forbidden fruit. Mr Grant told me about it. He read me the whole poem some time ago. You need to set about minding the business today. There may well be customers arriving any moment. Sarah has been setting everything out ready for them. And besides, I happen to know she has bought some fine mutton for you tonight. That will fortify you after all this reading.'

He looked a little strengthened by this, and seemed content to put aside the book for the time being and tend to his money and the business. I hurried out of the house, after clutching Sarah's hand and reassuring her about her father's renewed resolve, for I was now a little late for my planned visit to Mr Fountain. But as I reached the street, I turned back and peered through the window. Mr Laming was hunched over a pile of paper and coins, counting up his money and noting the totals carefully in his ledger. His usual old self is restored, I smiled to myself. You cannot keep Laming from his business for long. It may be that even he fell prey to the dreams and excitement of the last week like the rest of us. But he will be back with the watches and jewels, helping the desperate families of Cripplegate, in no time.

*

I hurried up Red Cross Street, with my mutton under my arm and my precious pail of milk, feeling comforted that I had been of service already that morning and anticipating with some excitement my conversation with Mr Fountain. It was clear that we needed fear no competition from Mr Laming and nobody else in Cripplegate had – to my knowledge – created such beautiful packages as we had. All my needlework training received at my dear mother's knee had prepared me to make the most exquisite souvenirs that could be purchased anywhere. So I was excited to discover how many Mr Fountain had sold and whether we were now rich beyond our wildest dreams!

The tavern looked very different, however, when I reached the corner of Beech Street and first could see it. Instead of its usual gaiety, with all the windows open and men spilling out into the street, drinking and calling out to the women as they passed, the doors were closed and the place was very quiet and apparently deserted. This filled me with more alarm than before since it seemed that my fears might prove true and that Mr Fountain had been called from home by some emergency. Mayhap some relative in the country had fallen ill and he had been compelled to go and offer assistance? But I had never heard him talk of any such relative, nor had he ever left his house to go visiting before. Or maybe there was another wedding or funeral in the neighbourhood that Fountain had been invited to furnish with drink and food again for the day? But if there was any such event, Mr Grant and I would have been sure to know of it as well. More than anything, I feared that our parcels of Milton, and the inquiries of Mr Neve, might be chiefly to account for the strange solitude.

But when I knocked on the door, I discovered that the house was not deserted and that after some delay, Mr Taylor, the surgeon from Derby, answered it. I was most surprised to see him, since I had thought that he was visiting but a day or two at most and had assumed that he would have been needed by now back in the north. He, on his part, did not greet me in the friendly manner with which he had consorted with everyone the previous week but instead drew himself up to his full height (he was a tall, spindly man – indeed I found it hard to imagine how he could have the strength to saw through bones and all the other necessary tasks of his profession!) and kept his thin hand upon the door as if he were about to close it at any minute. But I could see past him, through the open door, to where about a dozen men were sitting down at the table, discussing something earnestly together. Not a little astounded by this spectacle, I asked him what was happening. 'No matter, no matter at all, Mrs Grant,' was his hurried reply, and he moved to close the door again upon my face. So I pushed my foot through upon the threshold, to prevent the door from closing, and I asked him boldly whether Mr Fountain was at home. Again he looked troubled by my request, and as if he were going to issue another denial, when I heard a voice from the back region, which was unmistakably that of Mr Fountain. 'It's alright, Taylor' – said he – 'tell her to meet me around the back.'

I made my brief apology to Mr Taylor and the men for interrupting them, and retreated to the yard at the back of the building, where five days before Mr Fountain and I had embraced so passionately and shamelessly. He was already standing there, waiting for me, his arms folded across his chest and his face unusually solemn. I went up to him and touched his arm, but he remained unmoved, beside the barrels.

'I came to see what was happening, Benjamin,' said I quietly. 'It has been five days now and I have heard nothing.'

'I have been busy, Lizzie,' replied he. 'The tavern has been full every day, and I have been put to the test accommodating everybody and minding the bar.'

'It is not very full now' – said I – 'I thought it was closed, until I entered and saw those few men talking. What was happening?'

'Never mind your pretty head about that, Lizzie,' said he. 'It's just men talking, endlessly discussing. I confess I only understand the half of it. Mr Taylor persuaded me this was what I should do. Mr Taylor, you know, has come from elsewhere and is full of new ideas. It is politics, liberty, and other objects of concern which we know very little of, you and I, and you certainly must think of it no more.'

'Politics, Benjamin' – I persisted – 'what manner of politics?' (I confess that normally, whenever Mr Grant discusses politics, my mind wanders privately upon other topicks, for it is all too abstract and irrelevant for my taste. But now, since Mr Fountain was so secretive about it, I became more curious to press the issue more deeply.)

'Liberty, equality, fraternity. We live as slaves beneath a tyrannical king. Milton knew this, Lizzie. He risked his life for freedom against the despot Charles. *Better to reign in Hell than serve in Heaven*, Mr Taylor says he wrote. Men have been *serving* all their lives, says Mr Taylor – and he doesn't just mean in the tavern or shops or so forth – but the days of servitude and obedience are numbered.'

'You sound like these Frenchmen, Benjamin,' said I with some concern. 'This is how Mr Grant says they talk in Paris. But I am sure Mr Milton did not do all these things. Mr Grant never spoke

119

of it. He said he was a great patriot, not a rebel.' I blushed a little, for I remembered suddenly my conversation with Mr Poole, which I had repressed many years in an obscure corner of my memory. But I was more inclined to trust Mr Grant than somebody of whom Mrs Hoppey had been so fearful.

'Men will twist a man's words until a plea for freedom becomes an argument for censorship. But I have spoken too much already. Pray, forget about this, and do not tell anybody else what you have seen.'

I dropt the discussion, for he seemed troubled by it and in any case I knew that I had more important matters to discuss.

'Did you see the report in the *Advertiser* on Saturday?' I began.

'Indeed' – said he – 'very brief and misleading it was too.'

'Yes, I said as much to Mr Grant when he read it.'

'Old Nathaniel!' Mr Fountain grinned a wry smile suddenly. 'How has he been taking all this excitement? Not so easily, I should imagine.'

'He was concerned by the report, but was consoled by the thought that there was little in it, of information or veracity,' I said defensively. I wanted to focus on the most important issue at hand, rather than the rivalry between these two men or Mr Grant's greater sense of caution. 'So has there been any interest in buying the hair and bone as a result? Have we had any customers?'

'Nothing,' said he, feigning a look of indifference.

'Nothing?' cried I in surprise, for I knew that sales of remains had been happening up and down Fore Street, from Haslib to Hawkesworth, and that Mr Neve, escorted by Hawkesworth, had been making enquiries the length of Cripplegate.

'Nothing' – he repeated – 'I reckon the report was too general to provoke any outside interest.'

'Oh no, that is not true,' said I. 'Have you not heard that a gentlemen from the west end of town has been here these last three days, asking questions of all the participants about the disinterment? Why, he even bought a tooth off Hawkesworth!'

'No, I have heard nothing of this gentleman,' said he, again seeming a little scornful at the idea.

I stood there silent for a while. It was most unusual for him to speak so briefly and defensively, as if he were uneasy about some matter or he had a secret to hide. It might be, thought I, that he is nervous to speak of these issues when Mr Taylor and these strange men are close by. Perhaps he is afraid that they might hear of our venture and attempt to forestall us in some way. So I crept up closer to him, and stood looking up at him so near that I could see the ginger hairs bristling in his nose. 'I understand that it is difficult to speak at length about these matters now, Benjamin,' I whispered. 'Who knows what these gentlemen' – I nodded my head towards the tap-room – 'might hear or suspect? But you can tell me briefly now, very quietly, just how many of our parcels have sold and how much money we have earned thus far. I know that teeth and hair have been selling the length of Fore Street so I am sure we have sold many more and am anxious to know how much.'

But he drew himself up, and backed away from me a little, and said again that he had not sold any parcels but that if he had, it would be a matter of concern to him alone. I was so surprised by this reply that for a few moments I stood still, as one stunned. But then I gathered my strength, and I confess that I erupted with anger like any crazed woman in Bedlam. I shouted out loud, without a care whether Mr Taylor or the whole of Beech Street heard me, and I pushed Mr Fountain with all of my power. How could he declare that the sale of the parcels were a matter only for him? It was my business as much as it was his. I had given up the jawbone! I had fashioned the parcels, as gay and pretty as could be! I had told him the plan to make the disinterment publick, so that a better class of gentleman might want to purchase the remains! My mind went dizzy with the thought of the injustice and deception he seemed to be in danger of perpetrating, and I thought for a moment I might faint, but instead everything I

121

had learnt from watching the boys in the street came to my aid, and with a final cry I slapped Mr Fountain across the face.

Well, then, a complete alteration came over the man. He changed into the person I knew so much better, yet instead of expressing that passion with warmth and attempted seduction, he became violently angry in return. With a shout of – 'God damn you, woman!' – he pushed me right back against the barrels by the wall, so that I could scarcely stay on my feet, squeezing my arm until I cried out with pain. 'The parcels are mine!' he stuttered between pants of rage. 'Mine, to dispose of as I wish!' He pushed me again and I sank to my knees, more out of sorrow than weakness.

I was weeping by this stage, tears of anger and grief and bewilderment. 'But what about our pact, Benjamin?' I whispered. 'What about the agreement we sealed only Thursday last, in this very yard?'

'There is no pact,' he replied sternly, gathering his breath finally now. 'There is no agreement, and from this time forth it is prudent that we do not meet to discuss it.' With that final remark, he strode out of the yard back to the tap-room, and I was left, crumpled upon the ground, finally allowing myself the chance to swoon.

When I came to my senses, I looked about me. Two blackened faces of young sweeps, just finished work, were gazing down at me from the yard's entrance, but they ran off when they saw my eyes opened. In other respects, the incident remarkably had passed unnoticed. I was alone. But then the thought struck me. I truly was alone! I had been abandoned by Mr Fountain, cruelly betrayed by – by what? – by his selfish greed? Or by the baleful influence of Mr Taylor and his new ideas? Whichever was the reason, there was no doubt that Mr Fountain had changed, had changed utterly in just a matter of a few days, and that I was to be excluded from this novel transformation. It was this realisation that pained me far more than the loss of the reliques or the money. Mr Fountain had been my admirer for nearly seven years now, and I felt that I could trust him absolutely, and – dare

I admit it? – I loved him. But he had rejected me harshly, without compassion and with no recognition of our long friendship, and our moments of passionate intimacy. How cold! Nay, how callous! My raging anger and my despair racked my heart in equal measure, as I sat there, solitary in the yard, while the spilt milk spread in rivulets around my crumpled skirts.

At last, of course, I rose to my feet and dusted myself down and shook out my dress. I was not too badly hurt, besides a bruised arm and a grazed knee, and the worst pain was not visible. Mr Grant would be home soon from work, and expecting his dinner to be placed on the table before him. I could reveal nothing to him of the turmoil of my day, for the pact with Mr Fountain had been a deep secret between us, and to expose it would be to make open all the other facts which lay between us, the cutting up of the body and the market and, above all, the intimacy we had enjoyed. There was nothing more that I could do, in these circumstances, other than to cleave closer to Mr Grant. I was now alone in the world, without an ally and with scarcely a friend, and my only hope was that Mr Grant would retain his idealistic illusions about me, and nothing would occur which would disabuse him of that fantasy!

Adam explains the effect of his passion for Eve.

....Here passion first I felt,
Commotion strange, in all enjoyments else
Superior and unmoved, here only weak
Against the charm of beauty's powerful glance.
Or Nature failed in me, and left some part
Not proof enough such object to sustain,
Or from my side subducting, took perhaps
More than enough; at least on her bestowed
Too much of ornament, in outward show
Elaborate, of inward less exact.
For well I understand in the prime end
Of Nature her th' inferior...

(Paradise Lost Book 8)

BOOK 8

The evening after I fought with Mr Fountain, the hot, sultry weather we had been experiencing for the past weeks came suddenly to an end. A heavy storm hit the city, with rain that lasted more than twelve hours, and soon huge puddles formed in the street and streams flowed along the edge of the roads and the sewers overflowed thick and stinking into the side ditches. The roof of our house leaked, and so Mr Grant and I were awake half of the night, running with pans to collect the drips in different corners of our home. How grateful was I for this distraction from the burden of my inner feelings! How much easier was it to worry about the tumult of water, than about the tumults of my heart!

The following morning the rain had stopped, and a weak sun shone occasionally through the lowering clouds and the city smoke, but still there was much work to be done, sweeping out the clutter which had been brought on by the storm, cleaning the floor and scouring the step. Mr Grant left to work for Mr Strong as usual in the morning, after I had given him a bowl of porridge, and I remained, content to quell my thoughts with the tasks around the house.

Over the next few days, this situation continued. Mr Grant was more attentive than usual, bringing me a dish of tea before I rose in the mornings, and reading aloud to me – we were reading Johnson's

Rasselas during this period – each evening. He mentioned briefly that Mr Strong had appeared most cheerful and amiable since Mr Neve's visit, supporting his work and treating him as an equal once again, so that this in turn had affected his mood for the better. But after that, he did not refer to Mr Neve's inquiries at all, nor of course to the disinterment, but instead talked to me about other general matters.

Mrs Hoppey dropt by one day that week, as I was busy writing up our accounts for the last month – it had been delayed by all the excitement over Milton – to see how I did, and to give me half the payment for the grave I had dug for her the previous weekend (she retained 3d, quite reasonably, as her commission). I invited her into the house to drink tea, and she was clearly eager to tell me the latest gossip from the street.

'You must have heard, my dear' – said she – 'that a gentlemen from outside Cripplegate has been coming here the last three or four days, making inquiries about the digging up of Milton. He is a lawyer, and claims to be a great scholar and admirer of the poet. He even came to question me about it, but of course I could tell him nothing, for I was out of town that day. I said to him, however, that Milton had been a good Cripplegate parishioner, being born in Bread Street and finishing his days beside Bunhill Fields. That's where he completed *Paradise Lost*, I told him. No better place to imagine paradise! I offered to take him to the house, but he seemed unconcerned. All he would ask about was the disinterment, and then he persisted in asking me about the reliques! I declare, I know nothing of the matter, and wish to hear nothing more, neither. Milton is safe back in his grave, I say. Let his noble dust stay as undisturbed as all the other bodies in my care!'

'Yes, indeed, Mrs Hoppey,' said I quietly, while my heart was beating rapidly inside my breast. 'So do you expect to hear from the gentleman again? Do you know whom else he planned to question?'

'He mentioned that he was going from me to Mr Fountain' – says she – 'I have no further information about his intentions.'

My heart failed me completely on the mention of Mr Fountain's name, and I could continue no farther with the conversation. Indeed, I grew quite faint, and Mrs Hoppey was compelled to run forward with a cup of water for me. 'My, dear, the storm and the flooding, it must have wearied you entirely, and here am I, rattling on about trivial matters! How unfeeling of me! How inappropriate! You are always so good and patient with me. You should have spoken sooner, if you are tired. But of course you were always too modest!' She fussed over me, and cooed, just as she did when I was a young girl, and I allowed her to do this, feeling all the time racked with private shame. How false was her view of me! If she did but know my true sentiments! If she could but guess the real reason for my discomfiture!

It was the same with Mr Grant each evening. His mood was apparently so light that he even took me out on a couple of occasions, to drink in the Baptist's Head and to walk under the trees in Moorfields and to look at the new elegant buildings in Finsbury Square. Mr Strong was becoming more relaxed at work, he said, and he wished to make amends to me for all the weary evenings of neglect that I had suffered in recent weeks. So he took my arm as we walked in the fields, and we seemed as close and affectionate a couple as at any time since our marriage. But I knew in my heart that this was a deception. I suspected that Mr Grant was still troubled by the memory of pulling out Milton's hair, and that he was trying to push the guilt from his mind by taking me out for these merry frolicks. Occasionally I would look up at him and catch a solemn look in his countenance, a shadow passing his face as he recalled the agony of his regret and self-recrimination. He thought me entirely innocent, of course, a model of wise restraint when the rest of them were committing the act of sacrilege, and so his guilt was compounded when he thought of the unequal comparison between us. He was black, black as sin! And I was the pure white of snow!

The reality of course was very far removed from his fancy. It was I who was secretly harbouring a treacherous heart! And in comparison with my transactions with Mr Fountain, Mr Grant's deeds were as light as day! But how dearly now would I have undone those deeds and won again the undying loyalty I tried to show him outwardly. Now that Mr Fountain had betrayed me and that I stood to gain nothing by our earlier transaction, how I wished that I had played no part in the fateful business but had stayed true to Mr Grant's instructions to me. Then I could now be as really innocent as he and Mrs Hoppey believed me to be.

*

I shall never forget the day Mr Neve's pamphlet was published! It was a day that will be forever etched on my memory, infamous in my life's ledger, when I finally lost the esteem and affection of my husband, and the good will and friendship of Mrs Hoppey, the only other true friend I had the good fortune to possess! In one day, all was lost! All had turned to the cold ashes that I have tasted every day since!

   It was a week since Mr Neve had visited the parish, a week since my furious fight with Mr Fountain, and my anxieties relating to the enquiries were beginning to subside. Although there was a gulph of silence which lay between Mr Grant and me regarding certain topicks – the hair, Mr Fountain, his guilt, my guilt – nevertheless when we maintained conversation upon the common concerns of everyday and the pleasurable trips he insisted on taking me upon and also on his favourite obsession, the events abroad in Paris, then it seemed as if we were almost happy. Indeed sometimes, when I was walking through the bustle of the Chepe to the market, back with the crowds of busy, unthinking people, or when I was in St Giles' churchyard or the Upper Churchyard at Whitecross Street, digging another grave for Mrs Hoppey, I confess that I even forgot about the whole affair, and thought only of the excitement of life and death which had always kept me merry. We had heard nothing more from Mr Neve, or from Mr Fountain, and knew not that an account of the disinterment was imminent. On occasion, I even flattered myself to hope that everything would pass and that I would be permitted to continue living as I had always done in the past, tending to Mr Grant and not probing too deeply into my innermost concerns.

Everything changed, however, the day that Mr Grant bought Mr Neve's pamphlet. I found him sitting with it open on the table before him, when I returned from the cheese market in Milk Street. He was always a quiet man, but I noticed on this occasion that he was even more silent than usual, not greeting me as I came into the house as he was accustomed to do and barely raising his eyes from the page. I knew not the nature of the book at first, and so I busied myself with arranging the provisions I had just purchased, the bread and the cheese. Of course, it was unusual for him to be in the house at that time in the afternoon, since I would have expected him to work at Mr Strong's until at least after six in the evening, but I did not think too intently about it.

At length, however, he looked up and spoke grimly, 'I have just completed reading the account by Mr Philip Neve of the disinterment of Milton in this parish. Never have I read a more damning revelation of man's vulgarity and greed! It might interest you to hear the account, wife, since I know that you are incapable of reading it yourself.' He spoke this last with such unusual scorn in his voice that I was quite speechless with shock, and, pale and trembling, I could only nod my assent while stumbling forward onto the other chair.

And so he began.

A
NARRATIVE
OF THE
DISINTERMENT
OF
MILTON'S COFFIN,
IN THE
PARISH-CHURCH OF ST. GILES, CRIPPLEGATE,
ON WEDNESDAY, 4TH OF AUGUST, 1790;
AND OF
THE TREATMENT OF THE CORPSE,
DURING THAT AND THE FOLLOWING DAY.

Having read in the Public Advertiser, on Saturday, the 7th
of August, 1790, that Milton's coffin had been dug up, in the
parish church of St Giles', Cripplegate, and was there to be seen, I
went immediately to the church, and found the latter part of the
information untrue; but from conversations on that day, on Monday
the 9th, and on Tuesday, the 10th of August, the following facts are
established...

...When Messrs Laming and Taylor had finally quitted the church,
the coffin was removed, from the edge of the excavation, back to its
original station; but was no otherwise closed, than by the lid, where it
had been cut and reversed, being bent down again. Mr Ascough, the
clerk, was from home the greater part of that day; and Mrs Hoppey,
the sexton, was from home the whole day. Elizabeth Grant, the
grave-digger, and who is servant to Mrs Hoppey, therefore now took
possession of the coffin; and as its situation, under the common-
council-men's pew, would not admit of its being seen without the
help of a candle, she kept a tinder-box in the excavation, and when
any persons came, struck a light, and conducted them under the
pew; where, by reversing the part of the lid which had been cut, she
exhibited the body, at first for 6d. and afterwards for 3d. and 2d.
each person....

... Hawkesworth having informed me, on the Saturday, that Mr Ellis, the player, had taken some hair, and that he had seen him take a rib-bone, and carry it away in paper under his coat, I went from Mr Laming's, on Monday, to Mr Ellis, who told me that he had paid 6d. to Elizabeth Grant for seeing the body; and that he had lifted up the head, and taken, from among the sludge under it, a small quantity of hair, with which was a piece of the shroud, and, adhering to the hair, a bit of the skin of the skull, of about the size of a shilling. He put them all into my hands, with the rib-bone, which appeared to be one of the upper ribs....

... I collected this account from the mouths of those, who were immediate actors in this most sacrilegious scene; and before the voice of charity had reproached them with their impiety. By it, those are exculpated, whose just and liberal sentiments restrained their hands from an act of violation; and the blood of the lamb is dashed against the doorpost of the perpetrators, not to save but to mark them to posterity.

PHILIP NEVE

Furnival Inn,

14th of August 1790

FINIS

Mr Grant read the account without interruption, only looking up to regard me with a mixture of horror and sadness on two occasions, the first when the account described me charging visitors to look at the body, and the second when it declared that reliques had been acquired from Mr Ellis, who said that he 'paid 6d to Elizabeth Grant'. I quickly realised that all the information about me in the book had come from Mr Ellis, the actor who had bestowed the rose from his buttonhole upon me and pretended a great respect and courtesy. He had given Mr Neve some hair, with a little of the skin from the skull still attached, a piece of the shroud, and also one of the ribs, and told him that he had paid me sixpence for access to the body. I could not tell whether he had exchanged these objects with Mr Neve for money, but it did seem as if he wished to blame me for their existence, rather than his own unprovoked plunder.

My pact with Hawkesworth, therefore, had been futile, and the illicit kiss given in vain, since the story had come out through other sources. To be betrayed by Ellis! I thought again of his theatrical bow to me, and his false politeness and gentlemanly manners. The deception! After he had sworn me to secrecy, with his bribe of a rose! To tell others of my guilt when he was a voluntary participant and even a beneficiary! I had not urged him to break off the body, nor told him to take any souvenir at all, but now I felt that the whole conclusion of the account was directed against me alone. The blood of the lamb was dashed against my doorpost! Nay, I felt it burning upon my forehead already!

'I am surprised that my name does not appear anywhere in this account, since I am all too sensible that my part in this affair was both greatly influential upon the course of events and inexcusable,' began Mr Grant. 'I misled others who looked up to me for guidance! I stood aside and did nothing while they tore the body apart! I deserve the full force of Mr Neve's fury!' He sat silent for a while, holding his head in his hands. All this while, I was sitting in a state of shock, unable

132

for once to develop any strategy to confront the crisis. He looked up again at me. 'But I need hardly say, however, Mrs Grant,' (O so cold and formal suddenly!), 'that the portion of this account which disturbs me most especially is the part concerning yourself. From *Mr Neve*, I learn that you exhibited the body to anybody that would pay you a fee of sixpence! From *Mr Neve* I discover that you conducted them to the excavation with a lighted candle! Nay, you, to whose care the sacred body of the poet had been most solemnly entrusted, were the prime instigator of the violation of the body. Oh, this is too much! This cannot be borne!' He broke off with a sigh, as pitiful as any I had yet heard.

'Sir, I did not help them take reliques from the body. Mr Ellis and others took them of their own accord,' I protested. I had not intended to justify my actions, but the look on his face prompted from me some desperate attempt at self-defence, and the words sprang from my lips unbidden, unexpectedly.

'Do not seek to excuse your deeds,' said he. 'Shameful enough it is to have perpetrated such crimes, but to fail to exhibit the requisite contrition is beyond reproach! To think of all the nights since when I have chastised myself for not being more firm and fixed in my dissent, and lamenting the day when I yielded to some low desire and seized upon the great poet's hair, and all the while you were hiding from me the knowledge that, under your guidance, men had done far worst and accounted the precious body of the Bard as but a treasure trove to be bartered and sold.'

'Sir, I did not know the consequences of my action. Never did it enter my mind that these men would sell the souvenirs which they took,' said I, flushing a little with my secret awareness that I had turned profiteer myself with Mr Fountain. But this information had not apparently reached Mr Neve at this stage, and I rejoiced that, for now at least, my husband would remain ignorant of the full extent of my participation in the transactions. So even at this stage, I confess

133

I pretended to be more innocent than I was. Besides, I had made no profit, because Mr Fountain had betrayed me, so who was to say that I was guilty? 'I was all alone in the church' – says I, trembling a little to indicate my weakness more pitiably – 'and the men pressed their need to see the corpse upon me so forcefully. What, pray, was I to do?'

He softened a little with this. 'Would that you had listened more carefully to my instructions and guarded the body against all incomers! Or would that you had stayed with me and not attempted this high task without my strong support! I see now' – said he, sadly – 'that I had too high opinion of your character. I thought that you were able to withstand all temptation, that you had learned to scorn inducements and persuasion, and that the sordid matter of money was beneath your consideration. I was wrong!'

'Do not speak so harshly, sir,' cried I, giving way to tears that were indeed no artful deception but the inevitable overflow of my feelings. I had lost the high opinion of my husband, and who could say if it would ever return? 'I beg you, do not judge me so!'

'Speak these words I must, wife, for I blame myself for misjudging you. I should have known that all women are frail and timid, and that their easy virtue is no defence against the clever flattery of men.' My tears fell faster on hearing this, for never previously had my husband voiced such stern and bitter thoughts. Always before he was generous and respectful, wanting to know my notions concerning events in the world and talking to me as an equal. But I had lost that respect! I had betrayed that trust and had shown that I was as fragile as any member of my sex. 'If only' – continued he – 'you had turned to me for help when I visited you during that fateful evening, when only some of the men had plundered the body. If you had confessed, then, that you were failing in the task we had given you and that you needed my guidance, then I would have gladly have assisted you and attempted to restore the damage you had done. But instead you told me nothing! You deceived me, wife, and that is what I struggle so hard now to forgive!'

With that last remark, he rose to his feet and went to the door. He stopped there for a moment and looked at me intently, with a face so full of sorrow and regret that it pierced my very soul! And then he walked out into the street, I knew not where. How bitterly then did I weep! I sat down on the chair he had just vacated, and the tears fell thick and fast. I had lost the love and esteem of the man who I realised then – but o too late! – mattered more than anyone, who had believed in my ability when he found me working for Mrs Hoppey and had raised me up to be his wife, and whose good opinion of me was destroyed forever. How quickly, in just a couple of weeks, everything had changed! How fast my life had crumbled around me!

At length, however, when my tears ran dry, I arose and began to busy myself in the kitchen, tidying the provisions and scouring the stove. But I had neither the heart nor the stomach for a meal, so I just heated a little gruel and took that to my bed. Indeed I was so fatigued with weeping that I was soon sound asleep and heard nothing when my husband slipped silent much later into our bed beside me.

After eating the fruit.

... Up they rose
As from unrest, and each the other viewing,
Soon found their eyes how opened, and their minds
How darkened; innocence, that as a veil
Had shadowed them from knowing ill, was gone;
Just confidence, and native righteousness
And honour from about them, naked left
To guilty Shame: he covered but his robe
Uncovered more ...
.... They destitute and bare
Of all their virtue: silent, and in face
Confounded long they sat, as strucken mute...

(Paradise Lost Book 9)

BOOK 9

For many days after the publication of Mr Neve's book and the great exposure of my shame, my husband said nothing to me. He would rise in the morning and sit silent and apparently deep in thought while I set his porridge before him, and in the evening he would return from Mr Strong's and sit before the dinner that I had prepared. Afterwards he would go out, and not return until I was already abed. I followed him one evening, curious what he did each night and where he went. But I saw that he merely walked the streets, speaking to nobody and looking only at the ground in front of him. It was a pitiful sight! He had been such an upright, elegant figure, and now he stooped with bended head and slow, melancholy gait, broken in spirit and without fixed purpose, shuffling in a futile circle – Beech Street, Red Cross Street, Fore Street, Grub Street – like a ring of Hell.

The silence was the most difficult part to bear. I went out into the streets too, but not to tread a path of damnation, as he appeared to do, but to hear the noise and clamour of daily business, the shouts and jokes at the market, the cries of ballad hawkers at the corner of Fore Street and the screech and rasp as the knife grinders went about their task. So isolated and alone did I feel in my home with Mr Grant, that I needed to see that life was continuing as usual outside and that I was tied to this society by all the tender bonds of necessity and compassion. I could nod a greeting to a familiar face on one street and run to help a child who had fallen on another, and offer a word of comfort or a gentle reproach to the neglectful mother. In this way, I was reminded that there were other concerns in the world beside my own, that other people had their own small tragedies and triumphs with which to contend. But Mr Grant shut himself away in his own infernal suffering, not permitting me or anyone else to console him.

It was on one of my walks, a few weeks later, to cheer myself up along Red Cross Street that I came upon Joe Haslib, sitting on the steps of St Giles' with his shovel beside him, studying a piece of paper.

'What are you looking at, Joseph?' cries I, for I was pleased to see him, so fresh and strong he was and always with a ready smile.

He looked up, surprised that anyone should be startling him in this way.

'It's the latest *Public Advertiser*. My father gave it to me. He was in a rage about it this morning, cursing and shouting. "What about *my* rib-bone pieces?" – thunders he – "What price are they now? How many dittos do they have, you might ask? I will out-ditto any charlatan in Cripplegate!" I had no idea what he was shouting about but he was clearly so incensed that I feared that he might commit some violent act. In the end, he sent me out of the house, with the paper crumpled into my top pocket. "Go and find the author of this mischief, boy" – says he – "and tell him from me that one skeleton has only so many bones and no more!" So here I am now, trying to read the paper, so I may know what may be the cause of his fury and how I may learn whom it is that I am to seek. My father was too overcome with anger this morning, and I could not prevail on him to read it to me. But I confess' – here he blushed to the very roots of his hair – 'that I am not so proficient in reading.'

'In truth, I have difficulty reading too,' I replied, for it seemed a kindness to put him at his ease. 'Let us sit together, and try to decipher the matter.'

So we sat on the steps of the church, with the paper smoothed out upon our knees between us, and pored over the letters together, and this is what we read.

The Public Advertiser. Friday September 3ʳᵈ 1790.

A correspondent, passing along Barbican about a week ago, picked up the following curious bill of parcels, which we publish for the information of our readers, who may expect, after their graves are paid for, to lie quiet in them:

Ebenezer Ashmole, Esq., FSA

Bought of Timothy Strip-dead, Gravedigger to the parish of St Giles', Cripplegate:

Aug 3 1790	l.	s.	d.
To two eye teeth of one Mr Milton	0	4	0
To a grinder of ditto	0	3	0
To a bit of winding sheet of ditto	0	2	6
To ditto of shrowd of ditto	0	2	6
To a lock of light hair of ditto	0	4	0
To ditto black of ditto	0	2	6
To bit of wooden coffin of ditto	0	2	6
To ditto leaden of ditto	0	3	0
To finger-bone of ditto	0	5	0
To jawbone of ditto, with one broken tooth in it	0	7	0
	1	16	0

As I sell these articles on account of one of the Parish officers, I hope your honour will consider me a trifle.

NB. All the above goods are warranted, there being counterfeits abroad.

When we had finished sounding out every word and every number, and by instinct I had quickly calculated the account of the prices to check that the figures tallied, and that it was indeed a total of one pound and sixteen shillings, Joe turned to me in confusion.

'Who is Timothy Strip-dead? How is it that I don't know him? I thought I knew everyone in the parish, and the gravediggers most particular.'

'So did I' – I replied – 'I've lived here for sixteen years and I have never met anyone named Strip-dead. A wily rascal he must be, who keeps himself to himself and yet he succeeded in acquiring all these souvenirs of Milton, under my guard. He is the man you must seek, him and Mr Ashmole, who now apparently are in possession of the remains and wish to sell them again for more profit.'

So we sat a while longer on the steps, the breeze starting to blow the early autumn leaves around our feet, puzzling over the problem of finding the man that neither of us knew. Then suddenly it hit me like the thousand lanterns being lit all at once in Vauxhall. Mr Timothy Strip-dead did not exist! I jumped up and down with the excitement of solving this conundrum, until Joe could seize me by the arm and beg me to explain.

'Neither of us have heard of this man. How do we know that we are in error and the correspondent of the notice is correct? The bill claims that all the articles for sale are authentic and warns of there being counterfeits abroad, but it may be that this notice is a counterfeit and that Ebenezer Ashmole is trying to pass off ordinary bones which he has in his possession as the more valuable bones of the Bard, now that he has heard about our transactions.' I blushed a little at this, because I was not certain how much Joe Haslib knew about my part in the market of souvenirs and I was aware, by now, of how badly this action had become regarded. 'Indeed' – I went on quickly – 'it may be that Ebenezer Ashmole is a counterfeit as well, for neither of us have heard of him either. Perhaps the correspondent of the paper has invented the whole story. For besides' – and this was the observation of which I was most proud – 'who has ever heard of a name like Strip-dead? It is more like a humorous description than a name, a word to say what this character might do rather than what he is called.'

Joe looked puzzled at this so I tried a bit harder to explain, though I feared that I did not have the words to say what I had suddenly understood.

'Timothy Strip-dead is like a man in a story, a man in a ballad or a play at the Wells. If we had to invent an undertaker like Haslib or a sexton like Mrs Hoppey, we would not name them Haslib or Mrs Hoppey, would we? We would call them William Washbody or Mrs Digworm or something of that sort.' And at that we both laughed and laughed and hugged each other in glee at the thought of Mr Washbody and Mrs Digworm walking around the parish, arm in arm!

'Come,' says I at length, when finally we grew serious again, 'we must go and tell Mr Haslib the news so that he may be restored to tranquil spirits. We cannot let him go round in a rage at Mr Ashmole and Mr Strip-dead for much longer. His bones are still rare and precious.'

So I followed Joe Haslib to the house in Beech Street, and my heart felt lighter with this conversation than it had done for many days. If only all troubles could be explained away as an invented story or a humorous joke like this one!

*

On the Monday following, I was obliged to go to the house of Mr Cole the church-warden in the Barbican. His wife had sent word to Mrs Hoppey that she had fallen sick and could not tend to the house as she was wont to do. 'Go, my dear, and see what you can do to assist her,' Mrs Hoppey had said to me, when she greeted me after the Sunday service. The news of Mr Neve's book had not reached her in Fore

Street, or else perhaps she had not yet read the details thoroughly. In any case, I was greatly relieved that she made no mention of the affair or seemed to have any notion that I had fallen into disfavour. Her warm embrace in the churchyard gave me much comfort, especially since my husband continued his apparent vow of silent condemnation and sadness each morning and evening. At least, for a while, I had the consolation of my old friend in Mrs Hoppey, although I knew that she could not remain in ignorance forever and the consequence of her learning the truth about my character filled me with dread.

So on Monday afternoon, I ran along to the Barbican where I found Mrs Cole sitting up in bed, knitting and looking not nearly as weak as I had been led to expect. 'I have been plagued by the headache these three days' – says she – 'and I knew not where to turn. Whatever remedy I applied afforded me no relief. So yesterday I decided just to take to my bed. Mr Cole will have to fend for himself.' And she took another sip of tea from a dish she had placed on the floor beneath the bed and a bite of some nice rich cake. I looked about me, and saw everywhere signs of neglect and indifference. The house could not have been tidied and swept for many days, and the dirty dishes from many past meals were piled high in the sink. The stove looked as if it had not been scoured for a month or more and there was grime and dust on every ledge and surface. So, although I had originally fancied that I was going to tend the sick rather than act as the scullery-maid, nevertheless I remembered Mrs Hoppey's demand that I do whatever I could to assist Mrs Cole and I rolled up my sleeves and went out to the pump to fetch water for cleaning.

I think that in her languid way Mrs Cole was grateful to me for when she saw what I had done, and especially how gleaming the stove was after I had rubbed and rubbed it, she leaned out from her bed and praised my work and told me to come and sit by her and drink some more tea. I decided that her trouble was that she was indolent, rather than in great pain, for her conversation was lively enough and her colour was good. But I was lonely and in need of company that did not reprove me or remind me of my past misdeeds, and so the arrangement suited me well.

We sat and conversed for more than an hour about all manner of things, but eventually, inevitably, the talk moved onto the researches into Milton's grave and the great interest in our affairs from outside the parish following the reports. She did not know anything of my involvement, of course, because she had not read Mr Neve's book, and she did not seem to be aware of the men who were currently hawking their parcels, authentic or otherwise, along her street. In general, her lack of curiosity did not prompt her to follow up every piece of rumour and gossip. But she was excited – as excited as her natural indolence would allow her to be – about the attention that the parish was receiving from the *Public Advertiser*, and proud, without much understanding, that her husband had played some part in the affair.

'Mr Cole says that Mr Neve is returning for further investigations,' said she. 'He says that he might well come to speak to us in our house this next time.'

'Why must he return?' I replied. 'Surely he has published his account now and there is nothing more that he needs to learn.' My heart was fearful suddenly on my husband's account, for I knew that his only solace now was that his name did not appear in the narrative of the disinterment.

'There is a new story abroad that the body which was raised was not that of Milton at all, but somebody else. A woman,' said she.

'What!' cried I, hardly able to believe my ears. 'Where did this story come from?'

'I am not quite certain,' said she. 'My husband told me about it a few days after the publication of Mr Neve's book. He says Mr Fountain came round to see him and told him that there was a new opinion abroad that they had all made a mistake and the body which they had resurrected was not that of the Bard. Fountain said that his friend, Mr Taylor, had met one of his acquaintances, another surgeon, who had boasted to him that he had sneaked through the window to look at the coffin when it was lying open in the church.'

'The rascal!' cried I. 'It must have been the very same that I gave chase to in the church, because he had not paid the proper fee at the entrance. But he dived back through the window before I could catch him.'

'These surgeons are no better than butchers and not to be trusted,' nodded she. 'Why even last month, my sister was laid low with a distemper of the stomach and the surgeon diagnosed stones and took a knife to her and she lost so much blood that she was as near as dead, until the apothecary could coax her round with salts. And even after that the surgeon had the gall to demand his fee, when all she should have taken for the pain was some soap and vinegar.'

'But what of Mr Taylor's friend?' I asked, for Mrs Cole was in danger of forgetting the main story altogether in her distress about her sister, and I was still, in truth, anxious to learn anything that was connected with Mr Fountain.

'Why, I quite forgot. The surgeon was bold in his assertion that the body he had seen in the coffin was that of a woman.'

It was very strange. Of course I understood that a surgeon, of all people, should know if a corpse be that of a man or of a woman, since he makes a study of all bodies and in his training even learns to cut them up and examine them minutely, inside and out. If this surgeon was confident in his pronouncement, then this was a serious matter. But on the other hand, I could not understand why, if the surgeon had told this opinion to Taylor in August, and Taylor had told his new friend Mr Fountain, the truth should only be broadcast much later, in September, after the issuing of Mr Neve's book.

'In any event,' Mrs Cole continued, 'Mr Neve is returning to investigate the affair again, and Mr Cole is minded to allow a second disinterment so that the body can be examined by witnesses. I am anxious about his visit – I do believe that this is the cause of my headache, since I am governed so greatly by my nerves! You must know, Mrs Grant, that I really am of the most delicate disposition. So I was so afeared that my house was not fit for such a gentleman as Mr Neve. But now, dear' – she laid her plump hand on my arm – 'you have made it look so bright and clean, I think it is fit for anyone.'

And so she talked on about her fears and her pains and her nerves and her knitting, and I sat there smiling and nodding with sympathy, but all the while I was turning over what I had just heard and my heart was spinning. If the body we had plundered was not that of Milton at all, then all our parcels were worthless! All the excitement that I had felt looking at the coffin meant nothing. But so, I realised, did the weight of the condemnation which had followed. It was not such a terrible crime to cut up the body of an ordinary woman as it was to violate the remains of England's greatest poet. Perhaps my husband would forgive me and speak to me again. My mind was sent this way and that with confusion. Only on the Friday, we had thought that we had a rival selling the authentic remains but then we had realised that he was a counterfeit. Now three days later, Mrs Cole was suggesting that all our articles might be fraudulent because we might not have discovered Milton at all. One moment we owned something precious, the next it was claimed to be without value, no greater than any bone which I could have picked up while digging a grave for Mrs Hoppey. In the same way, I thought, might life be considered. It may be precious and true for a few years but then, if somebody should change his perception of a person or alter his esteem, it can become of little worth.

Then I recalled my home, silent and gloomy since the day Mr Grant learned of my deception, and my eyes filled with tears. Never would he forgive me! Never would our life together be as it was! Even if the investigation proved that the body was that of an ordinary woman, and not that of the poet, I did not think that Mr Grant would forget

145

entirely what I had done. For I had broken his trust. I had not told him about my activities on that day (and of how many other secret misdemeanours kept from his knowledge I was only too well aware) and I had not sought his help when the men were clamouring to gain access to the coffin. I had remained quiet when he was worrying about the reliques and I had not condemned the violation of the corpse. Nay, I had even assisted in the marketing of the remains and clearly not felt the appropriate outrage at the actions of others. In all these matters, I had shown my true character, as a person willing to betray and to deceive. And so it seemed to me that in Mr Grant's eyes it was I who was the counterfeit, I who would always be considered false, whatever the real identity of the corpse, and I could have wept heartily to think upon this conclusion, save that I must gratify Mrs Cole with bright smiles and good cheer.

Adam's agonised lament.

O miserable of happy! is this the end
Of this new glorious world, and me so late
The glory of that glory? who now, become
Accursed of blessed, hide me from the face
Of God ...
... O fleeting joys
Of Paradise, dear bought with lasting woes!
Did I request thee, Maker, from my clay
To mould me man, did I solicit thee
From darkness to promote me, or here place
In this delicious garden?

(Paradise Lost Book 10)

BOOK 10

To be resurrected once is to follow an illustrious holy tradition, but to be resurrected twice in the space of six weeks is, I think, a fate wholly not to be desired! It was agreed that John Milton was to be raised a second time on Tuesday 17th September for the benefit of Mr Neve's investigation. On this occasion Mr Strong was to be present and Mr Cole would oversee the workers (although Mr Laming was indisposed and could not be present, of which I will tell more later), and the whole affair was to be conducted in an orderly fashion, without the frenzied excitement of the first disinterment, when we were driven more by desire and wonder than by the cool, detached spirit of inquiry. I know all this, because Mr Cole applied to Mrs Hoppey to assist with the digging and the lifting, given her intimate knowledge of all manner of burials in the parish, but being still beset with the gout terribly, she prevailed upon me to go with the men and lend what assistance I could. I am sure Mr Cole was not entirely happy with this arrangement, because when we met early on the Tuesday morning I could tell that he was acting a little distant and formal with me, as if he were aware of my past indiscretions and was afeared as to what I might do, but I was determined therefore to shew him that I could heave a shovel and raise a flagstone on this occasion without any undue passion or immodesty, and I think, when he saw the results of my efforts, that he was satisfied with my skills.

While the men were examining the corpse, I was not standing in the inner circle so I did not enjoy a clear view but I could dimly discern, between the shoulders of the others, that the body had a more decayed, blackened visage than before and the whole of the lower half of his face was missing so that the figure looked more like a jagged stone or a rotting vegetable than the genius he once had been. Mr Strong had invited an eminent medicine man who lives in a fine house near St Bartholomew's, a distinguished surgeon who had trained at the Guy's School with the physician who has done important researches into the blood and – so Mr Strong told us – has discovered that it is continually moving through our body, pumping along our limbs like the rivers of London, the Fleet and the Tyburn and the mighty Thames! Mr Dyson was the name of the surgeon who accompanied Mr Strong into the church, and I recognised his tall, thin figure and serious air, from his occasional visits to the front pew on Sunday mornings. After Mr Cole and Mr Ascough had carefully raised the body a little from the coffin, Mr Dyson put on his spectacles, bending the wire arm slowly around either ear, and stooped down to make his examination, lingering especially around the middle of the body, although my vision was blocked and I could not see exactly what he did at this point. All I could discern was that he prodded in the box a little with his knife and that he had a measuring tape, so that he seemed to be making various calculations. Then he stood up, and said to Mr Strong in a loud voice – 'As I thought, 'tis clear it is a man –' and Strong beamed for a couple of seconds and stuck out his chest in an important manner until he seemed to recollect something and his face grew more sombre and his bearing more humble, and he shook his head and sighed, 'Well, we must then re-bury the remains, for surely we are looking now at the precious reliques of John Milton.' With this pronouncement, the assembled congregation gasped with suitable awe, and then Mr Cole stepped forward to supervise the re-interment, and Mr Strong and Mr Dyson led the important witnesses away. Ascough, Hawkesworth and I were left to lower the coffin again and replace the earth and stones.

'Well, this news will cause alarm in some quarters,' chuckled Hawkesworth, as we were throwing the dirt back down upon Milton. Hawkesworth always seems to take amusement from the discomfort of others, which is another reason I dislike him.

'What do you mean?' I asked crossly.

'They say there are some as has a particular reason for this body to be thought a women,' says he, grinning mysteriously. 'They say that if 'tis only a woman, then that Mr Neve will keep his counsel to himself. But now he will be up and down the parish, lamenting and moaning and condemning us all.'

I thought for while. 'Who is saying this, Thomas?' says I.

'Well, your friend Mr Fountain, for one,' says he, winking at me in a most annoying fashion. 'You should know. He started the rumour, him and that newcomer Taylor from the north. Caught them last week, plotting in the cemetery. Fountain tried to get me to join them. "It will be easier for all of us, if this Milton story loses its currency" – says Fountain – "and then Neve will leave us in peace to pursue our real business". But I said I was beholden to nobody, least of all a Northerner, so I left them to their plans.'

I disliked the hints that Hawkesworth was making about my friendship with Fountain, especially since now it was most sadly at an end, but I put away my private scruples because I was anxious to learn more.

'What's his real business? What is he planning to do?' I asked.

But at that, Hawkesworth grew more serious and circumspect, and looking a little fearfully at Ascough, who was someways off and who had not, I think, overheard our conversation, he whispered, 'For that, you must ask him yourself, for I know nothing about his real business, nor do I like to know.'

So for that day, I had to remain satisfied by learning only a half-truth, and yearning to know more.

*

I had not seen Mr Fountain since the night of our fight in his backyard, but I had continued to think of him each day. Even in the darkest times of my life with Mr Grant, when we crept around the house without speaking to each other and he shot withering glances in my direction, even then, when I realised I had lost the dearest companion and guide of my existence, even then I did not cease also thinking about Mr Fountain. Indeed, I think I missed him then more than ever, because his laughter could have teased me out of my isolated sorrow. But I had not gone to visit him out of a sense of pride, and also because I was not certain how I should be received. He had spurned me, and loath was I to provoke such an attack a second time.

However, Hawkesworth's rumours and hints had intrigued me, and the more I thought about it over the next couple of days, the more I was filled with a desire to know what secret business Mr Fountain planned. After all, I thought, it was just a few weeks past that I was entering into business with him, so it could be said that I had a right to know (Mr Grant says everyone is talking about their rights these days, and the world is collapsing into immorality and chaos in consequence). I resolved, therefore, to visit him one afternoon, armed this time with the expectation that a warm welcome would not necessarily be forthcoming.

I found him not in the tap-room, as I was expecting, nor in the yard at the back, rolling out the barrels, but sitting in the gloomy light of the back parlour, studying hard at a paper in front of him by the light of a feeble taper. His strong arms were flung out slack upon the table and his brow was furrowed with the exertion.

'What's this, Benjamin?' says I – 'reading? Here's revolution indeed.'

He jumped to his feet in surprise and looked most uncomfortable and tried to push the paper under a cup of porter beside him. 'Lizzie, it is a serious matter – you must not make light of these issues,' says he with a frown.

'Well, there's no danger of much light in here,' quipped I, looking at the small lead window which was covered with so much soot and grime that the sun could not have penetrated the glass for some thirty years. But he was still scowling, and I could see he was in no mood for humour. How changed he was from the days, just a month before, when we could laugh and tease one another with abandon! How different, even, from the day when we had wrapped the parcels up together, fired up with the excitement at the prospect of good fortune to come! Now he was sombre and even a little sad, burdened by some weighty knowledge or experience. I resolved to quiz him on this speedy alteration.

'Lizzie,' he said with a sigh, 'these are important times we are living through. The salvation or ruin of our country depends upon the right or wrong opinion and conduct of the commons. Each citizen must choose for himself whether he is going to stand up for truth and liberty or whether he will continue to live under the duplicitous tyranny of our oppressors.'

I was astounded for a few minutes. These were remarkable words and not related to anything I had heard before. How could he speak of the ruin of our great country? Was that the speech of a patriot? And who were the oppressors? For once, we were not at war with France at present; we had no enemies.

He continued, 'To delineate a faithful portrait of the awful situation of our poor distracted country, would only be to exhibit a scene of misery and desolation –'

But I interrupted – 'Stop, Benjamin! Who has been telling you these matters? These are not your words, I know for certain.'

'Mr Taylor,' says he, 'Mr Taylor has been telling me things and giving me material to read, and my eyes have been opened, Lizzie,' says he, pacing over to the closet now to fetch a paper lying there and brandishing it excitedly in the air. 'Now I know that some men are tyrants and oppressors and other men – the remainder of the people – are enslaved, although they vainly imagine themselves to be free.'

'What do you mean?' asked I, bewildered by these wild claims that did not address themselves to any particulars. 'Who is oppressing you? Who is keeping you enslaved?'

He thought for a moment, not expecting this type of questioning. But at last, he replied, 'Mr Neve, for one, Lizzie. He is continuing to oppress me. He is maintaining the constitution of inequality which is keeping this country impoverished and unjust.'

'Mr *Neve?*' replied I in confusion. 'You mean the man who wrote about our disinterment of Milton? The man who condemned us all?'

He nodded. 'The very same. Did you hear how he described me, Lizzie? He called me a "dramseller", a "ginseller", a "retailer of spiritous liquours". The scoundrel! Of all the most presumptuous fools! He believes that only he has the right to own a relique of the Bard, and that I, a mere dramseller, cannot appreciate poetry and have no right to the man. Well, I can tell you, I have every right and I intend to use it too!'

This, I realised, was the heart of the matter that was agitating him so forcefully, and I waited in silence to hear more, so as not to distract him from the purpose.

'Mr Neve came to my house last week,' said he grimly. '"I know" – says he – "that you stole pieces of that body last month, that you violated the precious corpse of Milton". "Have not you heard" – quoth I – "that the surgeon now has pronounced the remains to have belonged to a woman, a Mrs Smith of this parish?". "In that case", says he with a cunning smile, "you will have no objections returning the remains to me" – but I knew the game he was playing, and I was quicker and more calculating than he thought. "Why should you be concerned with the mouldering remains of Mrs Smith" – says I – "what is she to you, or should not I ask?" – says I with a leer and a wink – Then he grew serious and said sternly – "Fountain, we both know what is the argument here – I demand, in the name of genius and poetry and all the civilised arts to which you are a stranger, you and your ales and liquors, I demand that you give me all the remaining hair and bones from the body which continue in your possession". At this I grew very angry, for what right had he to declare whether I was civilised or not, or to make presumptions about my opinions concerning poetry or genius or anything else for that matter. For after many discussions with Mr Taylor, Lizzie, I understand everything differently now. So I walked up close to him, and when I stand beside him I am a head taller than he is, and much broader too, and I looked down at him and said, "I would not give you anything in my possession, not even if you were the monarch. No, not even if King George himself were to come in here and ask me for these bones, not even then would I render up what is freely mine and won by honest exertion!"' And Mr Fountain grew red, just with the recollection of his brave – and foolhardy – words and his new irreverence.

And I grew angry too, on hearing this. 'Honest exertion! Honest exertion? Why Benjamin, you deceived me over those parcels, you broke a promise, and treated me with scorn. That was not civilised conduct! That was not honest!'

'This is a small matter, and it does not loom large in the bigger picture,' says he, brushing his arm across the table, as if to clear me and all other petty annoyances from his thoughts. 'There are much more important issues at stake. The citizens of France have pulled down that detestable engine of slavery, the Bastille, to the ground and have established the principles of liberty, equality and fraternity in their country, and the time will soon come when we will be able to do the same here.'

'How?' I interrupted. 'How can you have liberty and frat– the other things – here?'

'Mr Taylor is organising meetings,' says he. 'He is reading papers and talking to people, and even corresponding with people in France. And' – here his eyes lit up with excitement and he forgot his feud with me for a moment – 'he tells me that our reliques of Milton will be most instrumental in the campaign.'

'How is that?' asked I, puzzled, for this seemed an unexpected diversion.

'Milton was the most fervent advocate of liberty and equality,' says he. 'He was almost like a brother in our cause. Listen, Lizzie. This is something which Milton wrote, which Mr Taylor gave me.' He pulled out the paper from under the ale, which he had been studying when I entered, and read slowly and painfully (Mr Fountain never was as good at reading as Mr Grant):– "*It may be well wondered that any nation styling themselves free can suffer any man to pretend hereditary right over them as their lord whenas by acknowledging that right they conclude themselves his servants and his vassals, and so renounce their own freedom*". Are not those magnificent sentiments? And they are the very words of Mr Milton of our parish, whose body you and I helped to discover for the nation! He wrote that! Taylor is proposing to read those words at the next meeting and then open our parcel with the author's hair and fragment of bone. It will be wonderful! The people then will truly be stirred to fight for their freedom.'

This did not sound like the same poet that Mr Grant admired so greatly. I knew that Grant would never show respect for anyone who supported the revolution in France. Indeed, he believed that the government should deal harshly with anyone who voiced sympathy with the French, for they were a threat to our peace and prosperity. And when I thought of this, I realised that Mr Fountain could be in great danger, if he continued to profess these opinions, and I sat down beside him and told him to be careful and to keep these thoughts to himself, for who knew where they might lead and who could be listening and what might ensue. But he stood up, drawing away from me, and said firmly, 'The only friend of the people is he who will at all times speak out and frankly say what the rights of the people are. I am not afeared, Lizzie. I will speak out, and I have the spirit – and bones – of Milton to defend me.'

I could see that he was not to be deterred, so I desisted from seeking to persuade him otherwise. But it seemed to me that somebody needed to be with him when he ventured upon this dangerous enterprise and that I could not stand aside and allow him to be enticed completely into the company of Mr Taylor and his friends. I had known Mr Fountain for many years, and although he seemed to have been greatly altered over the last few weeks, still I believed that he was, at heart, the same man whose flaws and fears I knew far better than did a radical surgeon from the North. Surely I should watch over him when he made his first speech, even if he seemed to be rejecting me and we were more separate and detached than ever. Besides, he was intending to use the bones that he and I had gathered together and carefully preserved and ornamented, and by what right could he expose them in such company without my presence? Those were my precious relics too, I reflected, and I should have some voice – or at least an ear – if strange men were to view them and derive some power from them.

But for once I decided to use some caution and calculation in my behaviour with Mr Fountain, so instead of expostulating with him about his purposes, I continued to sit calmly at the table and asked him merely whether the meeting would be held far from Cripplegate and once again to be careful about who might listen to him speak, for who knew what foreign spies and traitors might be abroad. This proved to be an excellent strategy, because in order to defend himself, Mr Fountain replied that the meeting was not far at all but indeed it was to be held at the Queen's Tavern in Newgate the following Monday, and that he had nothing to fear in any case. He made it clear that all conversation between us was at an end, and ushered me, far from gently, to the door.

Thus I derived cleverly the information that I needed, namely the location and time of the meeting, for I had formed quickly the following plan: that I would go secretly to the meeting myself! I was not entirely sure how this might be accomplished, without anyone recognising me or questioning me about my identity, because the men in Newgate often also walked down Beech Street or frequented the church in Cripplegate, but I was confident that in the next two days I would invent some cunning mechanism that would enable me to do it. If Mr Fountain was intent on launching down a path that could lead either to glory or to destruction, then so (I resolved) could I!

*

It took me almost until the Monday evening to devise my plot for witnessing Fountain at the radical meeting without being seen. At first I thought of going early to the tavern and concealing myself somehow in a corner, behind a screen or in a closet, before the men had arrived, so that I might view events in secret. But this plan had the drawback that I had no knowledge of the tavern or whether indeed there were such places where I might hide. What would be the consequences if I arrived there and either found no closet or dark corner, or indeed if the men were so filled with anticipation that they were already assembling for the meeting? Then I thought of going to the tavern openly and feigning an excuse for my presence, such as that I was awaiting a friend or even that I heard that somebody important was speaking and that I wished to hear his words. But this plan had the disadvantage that I knew no friend in Newgate nor was I ever likely to attend a stranger giving an important talk. Moreover I would not be able to excuse the fact that I, a woman alone, was sitting unaccompanied in a public tavern. What insinuations might be made! Even in my boldest moods,

I was still not capable of behaving in such a fashion or of defending myself against the inevitable embarrassment.

But it was late on Monday afternoon, when I was reaching my wits' end and trying to calm my anxiety by tidying the house once again, that the idea suddenly came to me. I was hanging Mr Grant's spare jacket in the closet (he has two jackets so that he can keep something respectable to wear in church on Sundays) and trying to smooth out the creases when the thought sprang up in my mind. I could wear Mr Grant's clothes and go to the meeting in disguise – as a man! After all, while a woman could not go to a tavern alone, an unaccompanied man was perfectly free to go, no matter how unfamiliar he was to the neighbourhood. The other men would hopefully not question me too much, since they would be too engaged in listening to the speeches and participating in the debate, and I could affect a cough or shyness or even – I thought rapidly – a stutter or other impediment which would prevent much easy intercourse.

The one difficulty, of course, proved to be the fact that Mr Grant's clothes were large and hung loosely upon me. He is a slender man, but far taller than I, and the jacket brushed my legs below the knees. The blouse billowed around my chest, but I was able to draw it in at the neck with a tightly knotted cravat, and the length of the breeches could be disguised by some carefully arranged stockings which covered the additional inches of cloth. The best disguise turned out to be his winter wig (Mr Grant has two wigs as well as two jackets, for summer and for winter) under which I was able to push my long blonde locks. Once I had placed on top of the whole the large hat that my husband occasionally wears, I felt the masquerade was complete. I confess that I spent a few minutes admiring myself in our glass, turning this way and that to view the length of my leg in the breeches and the swagger of my shoulders in the jacket. I even raised my hat and bowed to myself in the glass. 'You are a fine looking gentleman, Mr Smith (thus I had decided to title myself). I would be honoured to make your acquaintance!'

It was by now late on the Monday and I had to hurry through the streets to Newgate (I was lucky in all this business that Mr Grant was working late for Mr Strong that day, otherwise all this plan would have come to nought). Occasionally I caught sight of my image in the reflection of a window as I hastened past and each time I was startled anew. It was only just under a week since Milton had been transformed into a woman in the fancy of men, at the instigation of Mr Fountain and Mr Taylor, and subsequently changed back again. And now here I was transformed into a man, Mr Smith no less, maybe (and I smiled to myself at this point) the husband of the Mrs Smith whom the men had disinterred and examined.

The meeting had already started when I arrived at the Queen's Tavern. The room was extremely crowded. Every available seat was taken and there were men standing between the tables and leaning against the bar at the back and even huddled on the floor. I was able to squeeze in the back and stand in the darkest corner without any attention being paid to me, for which I was very grateful. As my eyes adjusted to the lower light, and the numbers of bodies pressed into the room, I was able to distinguish two familiar figures: Mr Taylor standing at the other end of the room, beside the man who was currently speaking, and Mr Fountain sitting hunched on a chair a little behind him.

The speaker was enumerating detailed lists of rules and orders and something which he called the Constitution of the Society, of which it seemed we were now all part. This speech appeared to me to be drawn out most tediously, but just when I thought that there was to be no mention of Milton or revolution or that neither Mr Taylor nor Mr Fountain would be given the opportunity to speak, the man stepped to one side and announced, in a different tone of voice, that he wanted to introduce a new speaker who had some stirring words to say and he prayed the indulgence of the collected company. 'We have indulged you too long,' thought I, but then held my breath as Mr Taylor started to speak.

'Gentlemen, citizens, brothers, the years of our oppression are drawing to a close. The revolution which we but began more than a century ago is now reaching its conclusion. Our forebears only partly achieved their liberty, when they turned regal bondage into a free commonwealth, but then they fled from that resolution when they invited the monarch – the tyrant Charles' son – to return. Now our brothers in France are shewing us the path to liberty again, where once we discovered that path to them. Freedom was the cry of Britons long before the men claimed it as they stormed the Bastille in Paris. Liberty, equality and fraternity was our lesson to the world which we must re-learn now again.'

The room was hushed now and every man was leaning forward to catch Mr Taylor's words. I looked at Mr Fountain and his eyes were shining and his ruddy face was flushed more than usual with the strong feelings that Mr Taylor was arousing. For a moment, I had a fleeting memory of Fountain's face, years before, as he had looked when he lay with me in the churchyard, but then I pushed that thought quickly from my mind. Nay, even I was feeling proud about Britain as a result of what Mr Taylor was saying. Yes, we would lead the world in whatever it was he was describing, and teach others the values and happiness we enjoyed.

'I have here the remains of the great soul who taught us the lesson of liberty better than any man,' continued Mr Taylor. 'Mr Milton gave us the noble, defiant words of Satan which railed against tyranny. He invented the sublime terror of Samson Agonistes in his blindness. He also penned the great defence of the liberty of the printing press and the Ready and Easy Way to Establish a Free Commonwealth. We need his inspiration and support now. And I have news for you. He is back with us. He has returned to lead us to revolution.'

At this point, Mr Taylor reached into his pocket and drew out one of the parcels that Mr Fountain and I had prepared so carefully. He held it aloft and pulled one of the ribbon ends. The cloth unfurled and revealed the lock of hair and a small, grey piece of bone. The audience gasped.

'This is a piece of Milton's jaw,' said Mr Taylor. 'This was the organ through which Milton delivered the immortal words of Satan. Listen to him speak again.

What though the field be lost?
All is not lost; the unconquerable will,
And study of revenge, immortal hate,
And courage never to submit or yield;
And what is else not to be overcome?
That glory never shall his wrath or might
Extort from me. To bow and sue for grace
With suppliant knee, and deify his power.

My friends, all is not lost. We have the will, we have the courage, and I think by now we have the immortal hate. Will you continue to bow and sue for grace? Or are you ready to overcome?'

The crowd roared its assent at this point. 'No more supplication,' shouted some. 'We are ready for revenge,' shouted others. Even Mr Fountain was raising his voice, and his glass, with the universal cry of 'Liberty!' and 'Milton!' Indeed I was ready to cry out with the rest of them, but I remembered at the last second my need for discretion, lest I be detected, and I changed my words to a snarl, as low as I could make it, and I clenched my fist in the air. There was a general agitation in the room. But Mr Taylor soon gestured again for silence.

'This is a lock of Milton's hair,' said he. '"*Methinks*" (said Milton) "*I see in my mind a noble and puissant nation rousing herself like a strong man after sleep, and shaking her invincible locks*". My friends, are you prepared to rise up? Are you ready to claim the liberty which is rightfully yours? See,' – and he held the hair aloft – Milton is calling you.'

Mr Taylor appeared a very different figure from the character he had presented to us previously. When he assisted us with the disinterment of the body, he had been willing and engaged and ready to assist in various ways, including offering some advice about the state of the corpse and its preservation or decay, but he had been quiet and not pushing himself to the forefront of the throng or leading the decisions. But now, he seemed to light up, as if a hundred candles had been ignited in his eyes, and nobody in the room could look away. We were drawn to his words, like hungry birds around a fishing trawler at Billingsgate dock, and even I would have been prepared to rise up with him and do I know not what.

But then the mood changed and my admiration for him altered to anger. While the men in the room were shouting their praise and their determination to follow him on his campaign, he held up Milton's bone once again.

'Gentlemen, I am most grateful for your assent and your support today. Mine has often been a lonely road to tread. Frequently I have encountered resistance or indifference, men with ears deaf to the loud cries of injustice and oppression and with hearts hardened against the suffering of others. But in the last few weeks I have acquired a friend who has helped me in my solitude.' (I looked at Mr Fountain at this point, expecting him to be named as this much-needed friend). 'Milton came to me. I was sitting in despair and isolation in a church in Cripplegate when a shaft of sunlight shone through the window and lit up an open grave. I followed the light and saw that it pointed to a coffin that had already, miraculously, been opened. There I saw the body of Milton perfectly preserved and still clutching a copy of *Paradise Lost* – thus I was able to identify the man – and his mouth open as if in speech. My friends, it came to me that Milton was offering himself to me, that he was presenting his words and his mouth so that I could continue his call for freedom. The shaft of sunlight, the already open coffin, the proffered jaw and book – all pointed to a fatal destiny, namely that I was the man chosen to inherit his mantle and to continue his vision. Here, my friends, is Milton in my hands. I am the new Milton. What in me is dark illumine, what is low raise and support.'

163

I was astonished by this speech. Mr Taylor had discovered Milton's body on his own? He was somehow chosen to inherit his reliques? He had not even mentioned Mr Fountain or any of the rest of us, much less the effort which it had taken to collect the remains or preserve them in the cloth and ribbons. I looked to Mr Fountain to see if he was going to protest but he was sitting still as if forlorn of sense, white-faced and staring at the ground. How could he sit there in silence while Mr Taylor told stories that were so far from the truth? How could he bear to do nothing while his new friend, who was the beneficiary of Milton's bones at our hands, betrayed him? It was intolerable to hear such a fabrication made public in this fashion, when the two principal agents who had preserved Milton for his use were present in the room.

So I decided that I must speak out, even if this revealed my true identity beneath the disguise. The truth seemed to be more important than my safety.

'B-b-b-but this is not tr-tr-tr-true!' (At least I had remembered my ploy of adopting a stammer, to distract attention from the high pitch of my voice). 'You have but to r-r-read the account of Mr N-N-N-Neve to kn-kn-kn-know –'

But the rest of what I was going to say was drowned out by the clamour of voices that arose in opposition to my expostulation and in support of Mr Taylor. The men pushed me against the wall, red-faced with anger that I might be questioning the words of their new inspired leader. I could feel their hot breath in my face and the smell of the quantity of ale they had consumed before the meeting began. They mocked my stammer, laughing at me. 'Mr N-N-N-Neve, is it? not Mr M-M-M-Milton,' one man boomed down at me (I was mostly far shorter than they, and felt imprisoned by a wall of chests and arms and clenched fists). 'Nay, is this boy a spy for that other boy Pitt? Is our youthful prime minister sending out striplings to do his nefarious business now?'

'You mistake me, sirs,' I tried to shout. 'I am no spy. I like liberty as much as any man.' (I was neglecting to stammer in my excitement and urgent need to defend myself.) 'But when I see the injustice of someone claiming a possession which came to his person by a very different means entirely, I cannot stand idly by in silence.'

But it was in vain. There was nobody to hear me or be persuaded by my claims. The men around me were clamouring for my expulsion – or worse! – from the tavern, and jostling me around the shoulders. For one moment, I caught a glimpse of Mr Taylor between the bodies of my aggressors, and I could see him looking most intently in my direction. I was almost certain, from the intensity of his gaze, that he recognised me, but if this is true, I am sure that it added to the pleasure of his triumph. For his expression was one of mingled feigned innocence and complacency, fixed by a slight smile and a confident tilt of the head. He made no effort to intervene in the tumult that had congregated around me, but stood impassively watching as if it was outside his control and unrelated to the power of his speech.

My view of Mr Taylor was obscured again as the crowd closed around me more aggressively, pushing me roughly between one man and the next, so that I could scarcely remain on my feet and I started to fear for my safety. Appeals for help or mercy were futile. My cries of, 'Have a care, sir,' went unheard. Then one young man – thankfully not the largest in the mob – landed a punch from behind upon the middle of my back and I staggered forward with the force of the blow, doubled over, and my hat and wig fell upon the ground and were trampled by what seemed like a hundred feet. My hair tumbled down across my face. A shout went up – 'It is no traitor boy! It is a wench!' – but to my horror the men were not deterred by the revelation of my sex and seemed to be ready merely to re-double their efforts to hurt me.

The situation appeared to be without hope, but at that moment I felt a large arm gather me to him and pull me through the crowd. 'Quick, Lizzie, I will get you out of here.' Like a bear hounded by the dogs in the pit, Mr Fountain forced his way to the door, as the men lunged at him and pulled and tore at my hair and clothes. As we reached the street, I turned to shout back at Mr Taylor, who continued to sit doing nothing throughout this commotion. 'Betrayer! Betrayer! You are no new Milton!' But Mr Fountain clamped his hand over my mouth to silence me, before I could say more, and pulled us out into the quiet of the street. We ran together, Mr Fountain pulling me roughly by the arm and I clutching the baggy extent of my breeches that now had escaped their careful strappings and were threatening to leave my female nakedness tremendously exposed, until we reached the corner of Beech Street and were able to stop and catch our breath.

'What were you thinking, Lizzie, coming to that meeting with all those men? Have you lost your sanity?'

'It seems to me that it is you who have lost your sanity, Benjamin,' I gasped. 'How could you just sit there while Mr Taylor spoke such lies? How could you have given him our parcels to abuse in that manner?'

'It is not abuse, Lizzie. You misunderstand the calculations of politics. These stories are necessary to inspire the men to revolution. This is what Mr Taylor told me. But women have no place in these concerns. My God, I thought you might come to harm in there! I dread to think what might have occurred if I had not intervened. Intervened at considerable risk, I should tell you, Lizzie!'

Mr Fountain looked decidedly angry, now that he knew that my immediate safety was assured. But I was angry too, furious at the deception of Mr Taylor and annoyed that Mr Fountain did not seem to be able to detect this.

'Politics or no politics, I am convinced that Milton believed in honesty, Benjamin. I cannot think that he would allow such a lie about his remains. I am certain he would not support a revolution based upon such distortion of the truth and betrayal of friendship.'

'Oh, what is truth, Lizzie?' Mr Fountain cried sadly. 'Why, you were yourself there disguised as a man, without telling me beforehand of your plans, and even now you are going to slip back to Nathaniel

Grant as if nothing has happened. If any of those men recognised you, do you not think it will be very long before he tells the story to your husband? What lies will you be able to tell then to save yourself from Grant's justifiable shame and wrath? What deception must we both now devise to avert that catastrophe?'

I had not considered this possibility until now, so concerned had I been simply with Mr Taylor's betrayal, and I was silent for a moment thinking about the likelihood of this fate. Certainly I knew nobody by name in Newgate, since my business had always been confined within the narrow limits of Cripplegate. But the men there often walked through our neighbourhood. I had recognised a couple in the tavern by sight during the meeting. What if they were to stroll down Red Cross Street in a few days' time and notice me? They could easily make enquiries about my identity and the news of my daring to speak out at a radical meeting could travel quickly through Cripplegate and reach the attention of Mr Grant himself.

'I will need to return to the meeting and ensure that the men forget the commotion,' Mr Fountain was saying. 'I will make some excuses for your behaviour, that you were mistaken or that you were taken ill, and quieten their fears that you were a spy or that there is any scandal to be reported at all. And I will endeavour to satisfy Mr Taylor that there will be no repetition of this protest and that I will support him absolutely, without this trouble, in the future. In this way, maybe he will be silent on the matter and the news will not spread abroad about your actions.'

I touched him on the arm to stop him continuing any further.

'Come back with me to Cripplegate, Benjamin. Do not go back to that meeting. Sever your ties with Mr Taylor.'

But Mr Fountain drew himself back from me. 'Do not seek to dissuade me from this course of action now, Lizzie. If I do not return to Mr Taylor, he will spread false rumours about both of us. He will say we are traitors, that we are opposed to liberty and revolution,

167

maybe even that we attempted to steal Milton's bones from him. In truth, there is no knowing what he may say. He is extremely powerful and men will follow him. You saw this yourself tonight. We could both be in danger if Mr Taylor turns against us. I must return. To be sure, I believe in the path of politics upon which I have commenced. I believe in the necessity to free people from oppression. But more than this, I realise now that I cannot turn back, that after this evening I depend upon Mr Taylor for my protection, for the truth, for my life.'

There was nothing I could do to change his mind. Was it because he believed in radical politics? Was it cowardly fear of Mr Taylor, which had also prevented him from speaking out during the meeting earlier? Or was it a noble determination to try to protect me, by sacrificing himself and returning to that violent and duplicitous meeting? I was not sure, since Mr Fountain seemed so different these days. Why, only a few days ago he had declared that he himself would speak at the meeting and rouse the men to mutiny by showing them Milton's bones. But in the event, he had sat in silence and allowed Mr Taylor to create his own, individual story. Men were so hard to predict, I reflected, since one day they could sound so courageous and the next, beside another who was more forceful, they appeared craven and weak.

I reached up, however, to give him a kiss.

'Thank you, Benjamin, for rescuing me. I wish you would not return to Mr Taylor now. I do not trust him at all. But I will always remember what you did this evening. Be careful, now.'

He turned and walked back up Newgate Street slowly, not throwing a backward glance once in my direction. I stood and watched him sorrowfully. For it seemed to me that Mr Fountain now was lost, lost utterly, and there was no remedy. The reliques of Milton, of which he had been so proud and for which he had hoped to illuminate a new heaven of possibility, had become the pawns in another man's ambition. Maybe radical politics (for which I had no real knowledge and very little sympathy) was not even the main purpose for Mr

Taylor's determining to adopt the remains among his possessions. Maybe he simply desired, through them, to add lustre to his own name. At any rate, there would be no place, it seemed to me, for Mr Fountain in the new commonwealth of Mr Taylor's vision. But from this banishment there could be no return. Fountain knew too much. He could not go back to his former innocence nor could he confide in any other authority to assert his part in the disinterment and preservation of the reliques. Indeed, if I were to believe him, he was now also tied to Mr Taylor as the price of his silence regarding my shame in the tavern. My safety was dependent on Mr Fountain's sacrifice and servitude. Whatever was the truth of this premise, one thing seemed certain. The burden of Mr Fountain's involvement with Mr Taylor meant that he was now committed to him, in oppressed and tortured silence, forever.

God's instructions to his angel.

Michael, this my behest have thou in charge,
Take to thee from among the Cherubim
Thy choice of flaming warriors, lest the Fiend
Or in behalf of man, or to invade
Vacant possession some new trouble raise:
Haste thee, and from the Paradise of God
Without remorse, drive out the sinful pair,
From hallowed ground th' unholy, and denounce
To them and to their progeny from thence
Perpetual banishment. Yet lest they faint
At the sad sentence rigorously urged,
For I behold them softened and with tears
Bewailing their excess, all terror hide...
So send them forth, though sorrowing, yet in peace.

(Paradise Lost Book 11)

BOOK 11

A couple of days following my expulsion from Mr Taylor's meeting, I resolved to visit old Mr Laming. Partly I was concerned that I had lost Mr Grant's second wig and hat to the stamping feet of the angry crowd in the Queen's Tavern in Newgate and I thought maybe that I might be able to purchase some similar items from Laming's collection of unredeemed pawned possessions without too many awkward questions being asked. I needed to be able to replace them before my husband noticed their disappearance, although in his present state of melancholy distraction I hoped that this might be some time. But besides I wanted to see how my old friend Mr Laming did. I was a little troubled that he had been absent from the second disinterment, because it was unlike him to forego any dramatic event in the neighbourhood, and indeed, when I thought about it, I could not remember the last time I had espied him walking through the streets. It might be, I reflected, that he is still buried deep in reading his book and forgets the world outside, despite my advice to him a few weeks before to leave reading aside and attend to the business. But I confess that my chief motivation in going to visit him was the attempt to push from my mind the distress, which Taylor's betrayal and Fountain's desperate course of life upon which he had chosen to embark, had caused in me. A good conversation with old

Mr Laming was just what I needed, I thought, to forget about the rough treatment I had received at the tavern and the disappointment about our parcels of Milton.

It was late morning when I arrived at Mr Laming's house, with its characteristic three brass balls suspended above the door, and I was surprised to see the place apparently closed. Always before, he would have been working by this time, whistling over his dusty collection of goods or cajoling his customers, who were often weeping when they arrived but invariably laughing as they left. But now I was compelled to hammer on the door. Laming's daughter, Sarah, answered it, a small child tugging at her skirt on either side. She was tired and pale looking, more haggard and worried than she had been when she bought the mutton for me at the Jewin Street market, with an apron that appeared to have been unwashed for a month.

'Sarah' – said I – 'I came to enquire after Mr Laming for I have not seen him for several weeks. But I see he is not working. Pray, is he still plagued by other distractions?'

She looked up and down the street – she seemed most anxious and distressed – and then pulled me into the house and shut the door.

'Lizzie, I am most concerned about him. Since we last discussed his condition a few weeks ago, when you were so kind to him and he seemed enlivened by your visit, he has declined greatly. He is at present sleeping within, but the untimeliness of his rest this morning is due to his having passed a sleepless night. Indeed he has scarcely slept this last week, but keeps watch throughout the night.'

'I am most sorry to hear this,' I replied. 'But why does he keep watch?'

'Oh, Lizzie, I know not the reason,' said she. 'But these last few weeks he has been troubled in mind and spirit. In the day, when he should be talking with customers, suddenly he will be struck still, his gaze fixed upon a distant point as if he were looking at something that is not visible to the rest of us. At night, he will not come to bed at the usual hour, but he will sit upon his chair mouthing words silently to nobody in particular, or he will walk about the house as if he were searching for something, his mind distracted and unaware of the rest of us. My children' – (Laming's daughter has four children, all under the age of six, and her husband left to join the navy a year since and she has heard not a word from him) – 'my children are quite fearful of him when he is in these moods and can hardly be persuaded to go to bed themselves, lest he wake them suddenly with his wanderings.'

'This is most unlike him,' said I. 'He is usually so energetic and punctilious in his business, and amiable in his conversation. But of what does he speak when he sits in his chair? Maybe in that we could find some clue about the source of his distress.'

'I cannot tell. I have tried to listen, but his voice is so low and his words so quick and sudden that I cannot fathom their meaning. But besides, the children are always crying and calling so much I cannot hear his sense above the din.'

I tried to comfort her, suggesting that it might be that he was exhausted after the long summer heat and that now it was growing cooler he might soon recover his former spirits. But at this point, she burst into tears and buried her head in her dirty apron.

'Lizzie, I fear he is growing worse. The last three nights, he has not even remained in the house but when I have come to look for him in the early hours I have found his chair empty and the door open. The first two nights he was to be discovered merely outside our house, talking to himself, but last night, I ran down the street and discovered him sitting in the churchyard at St Giles', shivering in his nightshirt and muttering away.'

It was very perplexing, and much more alarming than just sitting reading *Paradise Lost*, as I had discovered him on my last visit, but I thought that the behaviour must still be owing somehow to our disinterment of Milton, since that was the most dramatick event that had occurred in Cripplegate in many a year and Mr Laming had been amongst the forefront of the investigators. Indeed it had been he who had first suggested pulling off the shroud and seeing Milton face to face. But I was not sure whether Sarah was aware of our work. She usually only had time to think about her children and her missing husband, and today, when she was actually talking not about her children but about her father instead, she did not refer to the event at all. So I decided to keep my speculations to myself, for there seemed little purpose in airing them. Instead I endeavoured to distract her with my desire to find another old wig for Mr Grant and we spent some time rummaging through a large chest crammed with crumpled clothes and smelling sweetly of lavender to deter the moths, until I found a greasy, grey wig which was thankfully very similar to the one that I had lost and she would accept no more than two shillings for it. I declare that she is not half the man of business her father is, although her anxiety about his behaviour may have been clouding her judgement. (I was able to tell a convincing tale about Mr Grant needing another spare wig now that he was taking on so much additional work for Mr Strong. The replacement for the hat would have to be postponed until another day.) So after this, and a glass of gin together to raise our spirits, we returned more calmly to the subject of her father, and I told her only to lock the door of the house that night, for Mr Laming's own safety if he were otherwise to wander while under his strange distraction, and that I would call again to see how he did the following week. She seemed comforted by this advice, as well as by our drink, and after we checked together that the big key could turn in the old, rusting lock (normally the Lamings never felt the necessity to bolt their door) and that old Mr Laming, although regretfully imprisoned would at least be secure for the night, I left her with promises and reassurances that I would return.

*

Mr Grant was still not speaking to me at this time, but would rise in the morning and eat the porridge, which I had laid before him, in silence before departing for Mr Strong's and in the evening, as I said before, he would eat his dinner and then walk the streets alone in agonised meditation until it was late enough to go to his rest. It seemed to me that his wandering and isolation was not so different from the solitude and distraction of Mr Laming, at least according to Sarah's description, and that except that Mr Grant was able to go to work at the proper time and presumably accomplish his labours for Mr Strong as conscientiously as ever, and of course that he was able to sleep at night, albeit fitfully, except as I say for these provisos, his situation in his own private hell was comparable to that of Laming.

So I decided not to mention Mr Laming's difficulties to Mr Grant, not least because I was not sure if he would hear me, and also I did not want to burden his spirits further. But instead I resolved to bake several pies for Laming's daughter, to help her in her time of great anxiety and need, and I took them round, the last (an apple pie) still hot from the oven and wrapped in a cloth, the following Tuesday.

I think she must have been watching out for me, because the door opened just before I was reaching forward to knock, and she was standing, dabbing her eyes with the corner of her apron and sniffing all the while.

'Oh Lizzie, I have been wanting to tell you but I was waiting for your call. He got worse, far worse. I have been at my wits' end. I did not know where to turn – my husband being absent this many a month, poor soul – and I have been so weary and uncertain, and so in the end I just took him, that is what I did, and ever since I think I was right one minute and mistaken the next, and I really know not what to do.'

Her words just tumbled out of her, and I could hardly make head or tail of them, save that she was in great distress and that old Mr Laming was not at home. So I put my arm around her and led her to the chair and fetched her a glass of water, and after she had taken a few sips and I had sat down beside her and soothed her with gentle calming words, she was able to start her tale more clearly. It seemed that Mr Laming had become more difficult and violent after my previous visit. When he found that his daughter had locked the house at night, he became angry and would hammer on the door with his fists, shouting and calling down curses upon his family which was most unlike his usual behaviour. During the day, his fits and starts, which initially had been harmless but just a little strange, now took on a more menacing air, as if he were annoyed with the world for apparently plaguing him in this way and he wanted to punish it. At dinner, he could not be relied upon to eat his food quietly, but would one day push it away untasted and another day attempt to take the meat off the children's plates as well. All of this, his daughter bore most patiently and compassionately, until the last Saturday when he had, in one particularly violent fit, knocked over the kitchen table, crushing the leg of the second youngest child who was crawling around the floor. She naturally had started shrieking, and Mr Laming began to shout and weep, and then the other children had joined in the cry, and Laming's daughter decided that she could not bear this situation any longer. So after this lengthy narrative, with the digressions about the injured child and the puzzlement of the customers and the fears about the future of the pawn-broking business and Sarah's headaches during the week as a consequence, it all came down to this: that she had taken her father on Saturday to Bedlam!

'I knew not what to do, Lizzie,' she wept. 'I could not continue to live in that way, when every day I feared for my children, lest they be hurt or frightened by my father. But now when I think of him in that place, with the chains and the bars and the cackling laughter of the lunatics, I swear I fall into a deep despair. It is just too pitiful.' And she howled into her apron and I held her sobbing shoulders.

'I think they take good care of the men and women in Bedlam,' said I, always trying to put the best perspective on a situation, even though in truth I knew very little about the institution. 'They now have an apothecary who is resident all the time and can tend to the inmates and they have stopped the practice of letting the public go to view the mad for entertainment as once they did, until fairly recently. Maybe you are thinking of those bad times in the past?'

'I daresay you are right,' she endeavoured to rally a little. 'But it is the visiting that most alarms me. I know that I should visit my father, and I should very much like to know how he is faring in there, but I cannot bring myself to enter the gates. The place terrifies me. I tried to go there yesterday early evening, but when I was near enough to catch sight of that big, arched entrance way, with the statues of the raving mad, and I could hear the cries of the people inside, my legs shook so much and my head swam with dizziness and I was compelled to retreat. It is plain. I am a coward, and I freely confess to you, that I have not the strength to visit my father.'

'I will go to visit him,' said I, making the decision quickly. Somebody needed to view how he was accommodated and who else could go but I? 'I can tell the governor I am his daughter. After all we are the same age and look somewhat similar' – she smiled at this, because in truth she has a sallow complexion and has lost her plumpness since bearing her children – 'and he must be expecting you to visit.'

'Lizzie, I would be so relieved. I cannot tell you how glad that makes me feel, to know that a friend I can trust, a true friend who knew Mr Laming in happier days, will be able to see him and to tell me how they are treating him. He was always so fond of you. I am sure your visit will give him much comfort.'

'And I was ever very fond of him,' I smiled. 'I am certain he will be back here tending the shop in no time at all.' And to add emphasis to my declaration, I bent down and scooped up her youngest child, who was rolling around at my feet, and I bounced her up and down on my knee, tickling her until she laughed with glee. 'He'll be back here before you know it!' I chanted to the rhythm of the bouncing child.

'O Lizzie, do you think so? The children have been missing him so badly since he was gone. Here, I will give you some provisions to take in to him.'

She bustled over to the kitchen range, apparently to organise the food I was to take, and she seemed to move with more purpose and animation than I had seen in her for a while. Jars of jam were lined up and cheeses wrapped, and all the while she was singing and cooing to her child as if it were a holiday and we were going on a picnic. Thus it was arranged, that I would go to visit on Saturday, collecting a basket of supplies from Sarah on my way there.

*

I was bold in my replies to Mr Laming's daughter, because I wanted to put her in good cheer, especially as her situation with no father and no husband now to support her seemed so desperate, but in fact I felt far from confident inside. I had never been inside Bedlam before but I had walked past it often enough, out just beyond the end of Fore Street, and I had seen the high, dark walls and the entrance gates and sometime when I had been very close, I had indeed heard the cries of the inmates, just as Sarah had described. Moreover I had heard tales of crafty and corrupt gaolers, who would offer the unscrupulous a peep at the inmates for a large bribe, and of terrifying lunatics who would seek to destroy their visitors and take their revenge upon the world, and so yes, I confess that I was afeared to go there alone. But what could I do? I had made a promise to Laming's daughter, and I could not fail her.

I cast around for somebody who could accompany me there. Mr Grant was out of the question, since he never spoke with me these days. Mr Fountain was now as if lost to me, and my other friends – Alice and Mrs Hoppey – knew nothing of my role in the disinterment of Milton and so would hardly understand my private feeling of obligation to Laming or my fear that he might let out lurid details, in his ravings, of our shared experience with the body, which I preferred to keep secret. I was starting to think that there was therefore nobody on whom I could call, and how sad it was that my collection of friends had grown so meagre in just a few weeks, when I thought suddenly of Joe Haslib. He knew about the reliques of Milton – indeed he had even paid me tuppence to help himself to one – and he seemed brave and good-spirited to me, so that I felt that I would be able to walk fearlessly into Bedlam if he were by my side.

Joe readily agreed to go with me, without asking too many questions or pausing much for comment, save that he always liked old Mr Laming and would be glad to help take him provisions if he was going hungry in the hospital. And so we set off on the Saturday, with a basket of bread and pies and jam and fruit over my arm, and full of determination and brightness. It was hard to retain those positive feelings, however, when we drew close and caught a glimpse of the two marble figures over the gate, the one raving and manacled in chains and the other attired in no more than a loose cloth around his groin and staring with the devastated gaze of the melancholic.

'Do not look up, Joe,' I said quickly and we hurried on to the porter's lodge, where we registered our desire to meet with the governor. He responded promptly, maybe encouraged by the two shillings which I had pressed into the porter's hand to give him (Sarah had furnished me with money, to aid the treatment of her father). There was no difficulty in persuading the governor that I was Laming's daughter, for he had not been in attendance when Laming had been first brought in to the institution, and, since I had both money and apparently a servant (for so Joe presented himself), he was most attentive in his conversation with us.

'We have housed him in what I believe to be the most comfortable cell in the hospital,' said the Governor, 'but please, Miss Laming, do not hesitate to inform me if there is anything that I can do to make your visit more pleasant or your father's residence more commodious.'

He shook our hands, and indicated that we were to follow the porter up the stairs to the upper level. The building was dark and damp, and here and there the stairs had almost crumbled away, since, I imagine, so many feet had pressed themselves upon the stone. The porter stumbled on ahead, bent forward with a huge bunch of keys ready in his hand. The stairs gave onto a very long, wide gallery, with windows on one side looking out to the gardens and a series of locked doors on the other. These were the doors to the cells, we discovered, since each one had a grimy window through which we could peer in to view the person within. Many inmates did not require much peering to discern them, however, for they were standing just the other side of the door, their head filling the window and calling out to us in appeal as we went past. A few were chained to their beds, and could not move toward the door, and mostly sat staring dejectedly into space as if the world around them did not exist but they were suffering some private vision. But others were pacing around their cells, banging their heads against the walls and crying out with their pain, not the physical pain caused by their concussion but their own mental torment. We hurried on, following the porter, and I was feeling more and more a sense of dread over how we should find Mr Laming in such a place.

At last we stopped by one door, and the porter put one of his keys into the lock. 'He's quiet now' – says he, in a low voice – 'but if he starts to rave and shout, you just summon me by banging on the door and calling. I will wait nearby.' He indicated a seat under the window opposite.

Mr Laming was sitting hunched on the bench, which passed for a bed, at the far end of the cell. He was shivering greatly, although the day was not cold, and the thin, grey sheet, which he was clutching around his shoulders, seemed to afford him little comfort. His daughter had described his violent mania during the last week he had spent at home, but now he seemed to have lost all his energy and all his spirits, and stared in front of him in what seemed to me to be wide-eyed disbelief. (I learned afterwards that he had been bled several times, and thus was now in a weak and languid state, and that he had been doused by freezing water, hence his excessive shivering when we saw him. Washing with cold water is one of the therapies of the hospital, to surprise the mania out of the man, and indeed I witnessed just such a dousing as we were departing the infernal building and I heard, with a heavy heart, the melancholy cries of the patient – or victim as it seemed to me – as she suffered the discomfort of the wet and the cold.)

Joe and I stood for a few minutes at the entrance to the room, looking at Mr Laming and waiting for him to speak. But he was silent, and despite my attempts at greeting and friendly inquiry about his health, it seemed unlikely that he would respond. So eventually, not knowing what further to say, I reached for my basket and started laying out the provisions I had brought. At this, Mr Laming looks up, takes in the good smell of fresh bread, and crawls forward to look at the food more closely. I gave him a hunk of the bread and some cheese and he ate it hungrily, and afterwards he took some more of the ham I had brought and a gulp of the ale. I was not sure whether liquor would be tolerated in the hospital, but I privately thought that the mad need all the cheer they can get and if ale can raise the spirits a little, then surely that is better and more pleasant than any number of cold showers!

I think one of the causes of Laming's initial silence might have been weakness from hunger, because after he had satisfied his ravenous desire for food and had finished eating, then he began to speak in a reasonably strong voice, and I was surprised to find that he recognised me, and Joe Haslib too.

'Lizzie, I am so grateful to you for coming. I have had nothing but gruel this last week, and nobody to speak to me beside the apothecary who came to bleed me several times and the porter who brings my gruel twice a day and emits scarcely more than a grunt. I declare, it is enough to turn a man's wits, to be locked up alone for so many days!'

Joe and I glanced at each other at this point, as we presumed that the wits of men and women here were already turned, otherwise they would not be in Bedlam, but Mr Laming did not notice our amusement (I am pleased to say) and was not apparently aware of the irony.

'I never imagined myself to be shut up in Bedlam,' continued he. 'I have known a few others who have finished their days here – some customers of mine who have fallen so badly into debt that their minds have failed them – but I always thought I had the strength of will to resist any mental weakness.' (I was impressed that he was so clear-sighted about his problems.) 'Do not think that I blame Sarah, however, for I know that she took me here for good reason. I am calm now, but when the raving is upon me, I feel such terror that I must–, that I cannot–, indeed words cannot express....' He broke off here, overcome by the enormity of his fear and the difficulty of putting it into words.

I was afraid that the mania might return with the effort of describing it so I attempted to deflect him by putting my hand upon his shoulder to comfort him and asking him about the cause of his distress. This proved to have a considerable effect on his spirits for good and ill since he clutched my arm, looked into my face most intently and began his tale.

'It is Milton. Milton is the cause of my difficulties, Milton who has not let me sleep these last two months. You should know, Lizzie. You were there. You saw. Indeed you saw maybe more than anyone. But it is I against whom Milton most bears a grudge, I who have been marked out for his especial displeasure. Yes, indeed, I tell you, the *cold hand of Milton has me in its grasp!*

He squeezed my arm a little tighter at this point, and I shivered, as if I felt the hand of the poet himself at that moment, and not just that of Mr Laming.

'You remember that fateful day in the church we were all looking down at the body wrapped in its winding sheet in the coffin, and all we could make out were the shapes of the head and the chest under the cloth' (he continued) 'and I steps forward and pulls the shroud off the head and so then it was that I saw him face to face. I was the first to look upon the face of Milton when I pulled down that shroud. Indeed I saw the full sturdy chest fully out for a few seconds before it collapsed. And I stared at the strong brow and the square jaw. And now he greets me nightly, speaking to me directly, cajoling me, and reproaching me for violating him so. I cannot escape it. When I was at home, I would try to stay awake as long as possible so that Milton would not appear. But then he started appearing to me even in my waking hours, pulling at my arm, speaking in my ear, appearing in the dark shadowy corners of the room. So I tried to go out and avoid his clutches, but he would pursue me down the streets, no matter how far I went or how quickly I walked. I raged against him, asking him to let me go, insisting that I alone was not to blame. I even asked him to go and haunt one of the other perpetrators.' (I let out a murmur of protest at this point, but on the other hand I could see the justice in Mr Laming's remark. Why should he alone be the object of Milton's pursuit and not the rest of us?) 'But Milton would never leave me, would never pay any heed to my remonstrances. I supposed that I was most vile. After all I took most of his hair and was considering plundering one whole leg.'

In the previous days, I would have been annoyed to learn of Mr Laming's greed. So that was where all the hair went! Fountain and I had speculated much upon this in the early days of our business. But now, I heard this confession only with a sense of mixed relief and pity – relief that I had not been burdened with so much booty and therefore was not haunted now, and pity that Laming, who had only done what we all had committed, although maybe a little more excessively, was now brought to this punishment.

'This is most terrifying, Mr Laming. I pity you in your distress. But what does Milton tell you in your encounters with him?'

'When I was still at home, he was angry with me. I was at the receiving end of his ire and blame, and he can be the most fiery orator, most cutting in his satire and his righteousness. But now I am in here, in Bedlam, he is my chief companion. He has me in his grasp always, but sometimes now it is almost a Satanic embrace. At times, he rambles on with his interminable sentences that I can never follow because they do not follow the normal order of natural communication. But at other times, he murmurs, over and over again,

Me miserable! Which way shall I fly

Infinite wrath and infinite despair?

Which way I fly is Hell; myself am Hell.

And I have learned to repeat with him, 'Which way I fly is Hell; myself am Hell,' until I cannot distinguish my voice from Milton's, and it seems that we are in Hell together in an infernal embrace, his cold hands about me and my face smothered in his long, damp hair.'

I turned and looked at Joe Haslib at this point, and he was crouching stock still on the floor, his eyes staring in terror and his mouth hanging open. I confess that my own blood was running cold and my breath was going in and out in short, fragmented bursts. I stood up, pulling Joe to his feet. But Mr Laming was growing more agitated in his raving, muttering 'myself am Hell' in louder and more aggressive tones and rising to stand quite close to us.

'Here is the cold hand of Milton,' he snarled, his gnarled fingers moving towards us. 'Myself am Hell. See the hand stretches towards you, haunting your days and chilling your nights. Myself am Hell. The hand has me in its grasp. Myself am Hell. It will grasp you!'

He leapt forward and seized me around the throat. Joe hammered on the door and yelled for all he was worth, shouting for the porter to rescue us, and a moment later the door was unlocked, the porter had succeeded in releasing me from Laming's clutches and I was pulled outside and the door slammed upon Laming's ragings. Joe and I could hear him just the other side of the door, beating it with his fist and shouting that 'he was coming', but whether Laming meant himself or Milton by this, or even the devil himself, we knew not.

I was in a considerable state of shock by these events and accepted the assistance of the porter and Joe Haslib to move to the window seat across the gallery to recover. It was all most unexpected for, during the bulk of the conversation, Laming had acted so calmly and courteously, explaining to us logically the cause of his distress. But then it was as if he had been overtaken by a demonic spirit – I hesitate to name it the spirit of Milton, despite Laming's own assertion, for Milton should scarcely be considered so malignant – a demonic spirit which called him to act so violently, and indeed he had been almost at the point of suffocating me, if the porter had not come so swiftly to my aid. And this the man who had once treated me almost like a daughter! It was a terrifying transformation indeed.

At last Mr Laming's hammering on the door ceased, and it seemed that his rage had died down, and thus it was easier for us to resume our normal calm and resolve. I realised that my basket as well as the additional blanket I had brought had been left flung down upon the floor, but I reflected that Laming would discover these things when he was in quieter mood and enjoy the benefit of them. And so we left him and departed, with no more incidents save, as I said earlier, witnessing the disturbing dousing of one of the other patients a few cells down the corridor.

I still had the duty of reporting back to Laming's daughter the details of our visit and in what condition we had found her father. But it seemed to me that an accurate description of all that had transpired was not beneficial to her in any way. So I told her simply that he had been grateful for the food and that he retained a healthy appetite, that he was kept clean and well attended by the apothecary and the porter and that the violence of his mania, which she had witnessed at home, seemed to have abated. 'He does not blame you at all for his incarceration but he sits quietly on his bed and contemplates poetry, and thus he seems to find companionship and consolation,' I told her, half truthfully, and she seemed contented with this account, almost ready to believe that he would soon stand beside her in the pawn shop, engaging in the banter with the customers which she was now struggling to continue.

I swore Joe Haslib to absolute secrecy about the visit, and I myself told no one. Indeed, as I have said, there was hardly anyone remaining to whom I could tell the tale. But for many nights afterwards I dreamed about the event, about Laming's hand coming towards my throat, and mostly it was the hand of the pawnbroker that stretched towards me but just occasionally it was the cold hand of Milton himself, with the whispered words, 'Myself am Hell! Myself am Hell!'

Expulsion from Eden.

They looking back, all th' eastern side beheld
Of Paradise, so late their happy seat,
Waved over by that flaming brand, the gate
With dreadful faces thronged and fiery arms:
Some natural tears they dropped, but wiped them soon;
The world was all before them, where to choose
Their place of rest, and Providence their guide:
They hand in hand with wand'ring steps and slow,
Through Eden took their solitary way.

(Paradise Lost Book 12)

BOOK 12

I remember the day that the second edition of Mr Neve's book was published, for it prompted the final breaking of his silence by Mr Grant. He arrived back at the house early, as I was engaged in pickling the pears I had bought earlier that day from a barrow at the corner of Fore Street. The house was reeking of vinegar, and I was standing slicing and stirring and thinking to myself that perhaps when we ate these pears in the cold evenings the following February Mr Grant might still not be saying one word to me and we would be slipping the sharp biting fruit down our throats in angry, resentful silence. In past years he loved my pickled pears so much he would laugh and talk and our winter evenings would feel like summer again with the golden fruit as luminous as the hidden sun. But maybe this coming February the pears would bring back only the bitter memories of these dark days that were so full of distrust and disappointment. So I was thinking these sad thoughts when he walked in and threw down the book upon the table.

'Mr Neve has pronounced most definitely at last! The body was indeed that of Milton,' said he.

I looked up, drying my hands on a cloth, and ran forward and took his hand anxiously and wept tears, but whether they were of joy at hearing his voice addressing me finally or of remorse at hearing that we had indeed violated his favourite poet, I knew not which. But he led me to the chair gently, and set me down, and read to me the whole account, from first title to final postscript.

A
NARRATIVE
OF THE
DISINTERMENT
OF
MILTON'S COFFIN,
IN THE
PARISH-CHURCH OF ST. GILES, CRIPPLEGATE,
ON WEDNESDAY, 4ᵀᴴ OF AUGUST, 1790;
AND OF
THE TREATMENT OF THE CORPSE,
DURING THAT AND THE FOLLOWING DAY.

THE SECOND EDITION, WITH ADDITIONS.

....In recording a transaction, which will strike every liberal mind with horror and disgust, I cannot omit to declare, that I have procured those relics, which I possess, only in hope of bearing part in a pious and honourable restitution of all that has been taken; the sole atonement, which can now be made, to the violated rights of the dead; to the insulted parishioners at large; and to the feelings of all good men.

POSTSCRIPT

As some reports have been circulated, and some anonymous papers have appeared, since the publication of this pamphlet, with intent to induce a belief that the corpse mentioned in it is that of a woman, and as the curiosity of the public now calls for a second impression of it, an opportunity is offered of relating a few circumstances, which have happened since 14th of August, and which, in some degree, may confirm the opinion that the corpse is that of Milton" .... It is, therefore, to be believed, that the unworthy treatment, on the 4th, was offered to the corpse of Milton. Knowing what I know, I must not be silent. It is a very unpleasing story to relate; but, as it has fallen to my task, I will not shrink from it. I respect nothing in this world more than truth and the memory of Milton; and to swerve in a tittle from the first would offend the latter. I shall give the plain and simple narrative, as delivered by the parties themselves; if it sit heavy on any of their shoulders, it is a burthen of their own taking up and their own backs must bear it. They are all, as I find, very fond of deriving honour to themselves from Milton, as their parishioner; perhaps the mode, which I have hinted, is the only one, which they have now left themselves, of proving an equal desire to do honour to him. If I had thought that in personally proposing to the parish-officers a general search for and collection of all the spoils, and to put them, together with the mangled corpse and old coffin, into a new leaden one, I should have been attended to, I would have taken that method; but when I found such impertinent inventions, as setting up a fabulous surgeon to creep-in at a window, practised, I felt that so low an attempt at derision would ensure that whatever I should afterwards propose would be equally derided, and I had then left no other means than to call in the public opinion in aid of my own, and to hope that we should at length see the bones of an honest man, and the first scholar and poet our country can boast, restored to their sepulchre.

Philip Neve 8th of Oct 1790

When he had finished reading, Mr Grant took off his spectacles and spoke to me most slowly and firmly.

'The corpse we dug up was not that of a woman, as some scurrilous rumour would have it, but that of our greatest poet, just as I said from the beginning. We bear the most grievous responsibility for the violation.

Our task is therefore clear to me. Mr Neve indicates as much at the end of his tract. We must return any items in our possession or that of our associates to him. He will restore the remains to the grave. Only by doing this can we begin to make amends for what we did and hope to get some absolution.'

I thought for a moment, but I was so inclined to do anything that would please my husband and restore me to his approval that I accepted his proposal without demur, and told him, not without a pang or two in the heart, that I had given all my reliques to Mr Fountain and I knew not what he did with them now. Was this treachery after the promise that Mr Fountain had extracted from me not to reveal his continued possession of the bones nor his future plans for them? I do not know. My husband demanded my confession and loyalty to him, so I duly obeyed him, but I felt some unease as I waited for his response.

'No matter, it is for Fountain to examine his own conscience and respond to the appeal of Neve in his book,' says my husband, and I sank back with relief, for there was therefore no need for me to return again to Fountain's house and confront him. Indeed, though my husband knew it not, Fountain probably was no longer free to make any decisions regarding the reliques, since they were now under the authority of Mr Taylor, to whom Fountain was bound, in silent obligation, possibly forever.

'And what of Mr Laming, who I also understand is in possession of the hair?' I blushed a little as I asked this, for I did not know if my husband was aware of Laming's current incarceration in Bedlam. I had not ventured back to the institution since my visit that I have described, but I thought about the poor man frequently and it was enough to make me turn cold with fear. Laming was not at liberty to do anything about the remains or indeed any other business, and his days of walking freely around Cripplegate might never return.

'Again, I cannot be responsible for the actions of Laming,' said Mr Grant. 'And I gather too that he has his own difficulties with which to contend at present.' And he said no more upon the subject so I knew not to what extent he was apprised of the full nature of Laming's 'difficulties'.

But then he went off to the closet and came back with a parcel, wrapped in an old issue of the *Advertiser*. He opened the paper, and I saw the large clump of hair coiled there, just as he had seized it on the fateful morning in August. 'I have thought of little else since,' he whispers in agonised tones. 'Just this hair and your betrayal, Lizzie. Now if you yourself restore this to Mr Neve, maybe both wounds may be healed.'

'I must return it?' gasped I – 'but how? Where?'

'I believe he resides in Furnival's Inn, in Holborn. You could walk there tomorrow afternoon. In this way, you could return these precious locks of hair to this most civilised and scholarly man, who is best able to protect them, and you could restore yourself to my full confidence and trust. We are shut out from Paradise but the world lies all before us, after all,' he finished with a wry smile.

There was no dissuading him once his mind was resolved upon a matter, so the next afternoon I set out up the hill at Farringdon and along the new street to Holborn, and all the time as I walked the air became fresher and the streets quieter and more ordered and the houses larger and more impenetrable to the curious gaze. I had never spoken directly to a wealthy gentleman before, nor had I ventured alone so far from Cripplegate or so far west, and my heart beat quicker with anxiety and trepidation. I knew that I would recognise Mr Neve, for I had seen his slight, well-dressed figure passing the churchyard during his investigation, but he had never knowingly laid eyes on me and I was not certain how he would receive me, and whether he would castigate me for my transgression and lecture me upon my folly, in the way in which he did in his book, or whether in person he would assume the gentle, civilised manner which my husband described. 'Take courage, Lizzie,' says I to myself as I walked, marvelling at the smooth flagged pavement and the carriages occasionally rattling past. 'This is but a small matter compared to the deeds you have done before.

Be confident, and you can win him to your cause.'

I was not certain whether I would be able to find the building, but once I reached High Holborn I asked a sweep who was hurrying by – I did not dare to stop the carriages or their passengers who occasionally disembarked in front of me – and he looked at me as if I were a fool or a country girl at least and nodded over at the imposing façade of windows and shutters and columns that stretched the length of the road. I had thought that that edifice was a whole street and not just one building but with his cheeky 'you are looking at it, love! – that's Furnival's,' he was gone, and I swallowed hard and crossed over to the large, arched entrance way.

Inside there was a great inner courtyard, open to the sky, with buildings surrounding it on all sides, some with big gable windows overhanging the cobbled ground below, and others with steep wooden stairs leading up to what I supposed were the entrances to men's homes. Fortunately there was considerable bustle in the courtyard, with men and women coming and going and a few horses being led to the stable in one corner, their clattering hooves echoing off the high timber walls.

'You should speak to the doorman, lass,' shouted one ostler at me as he hurried past, pulling the bridle of a sleek-looking horse. 'He will tell you where to go. He's really the master of this establishment.' And he pointed to the door beside the staircase on the opposite side of the court.

'I wish to speak to Mr Neve, Mr Philip Neve,' said I to the doorman, once I had found his office, piled high with uncollected mail and papers and heavy bunches of keys.

'Ah Mr Neve,' says he, drawing himself up to his full height, which was scarcely greater than my own. 'And who might I say is his visitor? Is he expecting you?'

'My name is Elizabeth Grant, *Mrs* Elizabeth Grant,' says I, eager to show that I was a respectable married woman. 'I am afraid that he is not expecting me. But I have business to discuss with him which I am certain will interest him most particularly.'

'Business, you say,' said he. 'I did not know that Mr Neve did *business* with women in the afternoons.' But he left his station at the foot of the staircase and indicated that I was to follow him to the upper level.

After I was shown up to Mr Neve's rooms by the old doorman, who leered at me over his spectacles and made far too many saucy hints and asides about my *business* in my opinion, I found the gentleman sitting at his desk, surrounded by books and papers, and writing furiously. I had never seen such a large, spacious room, lit by two broad windows, looking out onto the street, which were so generous and bright that there was no need for any lantern or smoking candle on the desk to afford sufficient light for reading and a person could walk a good many paces up and down the room without encountering any obstacle. For a moment, I trembled to find myself in such elegant circumstances, and I was struck dumb to think how far I had come since the days I served Mrs Hoppey.

Mr Neve looked up in surprise when I entered, and I recovered my boldness and dropt a curtsey and said, ever so politely, that, 'I am come from Cripplegate, sir, to return the reliques of Milton, and to ask for the blood of the lamb to be wiped from our doorpost,' and I held out the clump of hair, which was damp and sticky in my hand. He laughed, most unexpectedly and kindly, and beckoned me forward to explain to him who I was and how I came to be in this situation (not before taking the hair and placing it reverently in a drawer in his desk). So I started to tell him this narrative, and after a while, when he realised that it was not a short tale that I had to recount, he called for the tea-table to be brought in, and we sat down together to drink tea, and he even brought out paper and ink to make notes. As he wrote, scratching quickly with his pen, he furrowed his brow and his spectacles slipped down his fine bony nose, a little like Mr Grant's, and I was impressed by his scholarly knowledge and the wise nature of his questions, and I found myself revealing more and more of the story until I was telling him facts which I had never acknowledged to anyone, not even Mr

Grant or Mr Fountain. And all the while his eyes sparkled and looked encouraging rather than wrathful or chastising, and I grew round and expansive in my telling.

At last, he leaned back in his chair, and looked me up and down most intently, and asked me specifically my age and my inclinations and what was my interest in the poet Milton, and I confessed that I knew that he was a genius, because many people had told me so, but that I regretted that I could not read a word.

'Do you mean to say,' said Mr Neve, 'that you have never learned to read or write?'

'It is not on account of the neglect of others,' I replied. 'Mrs Hoppey sent me to school one day a week, but I always found numbers easier than words.'

'Ah' – said he – 'it depends which words you read. Maybe the words of a school primer are not inspiring, but if you were to read the words of poets together with somebody who truly understands them, then it would be a different matter.'

After this, he suggested that, if it was agreeable to me and acceptable to my husband, he could teach me to read Milton's works, if I came to visit him each Friday and brought him fish from the market. For on Fridays, he said, the regular housekeeper who prepared his dinners was away, and he was partial to fresh fish on a Friday. I was overwhelmed with excitement at the prospect of this plan, for the hour seemed to be dawning when the whole world of poetry would be opened to my eyes and I would be able to sit down with Mr Grant and converse with him about matters which stirred his heart, and so I took a deep breath, and I whispered that I liked Mr Neve's proposal very well indeed, and I was ready to come down the very next Friday, with as fresh a fish in Billingsgate as I could find. I was sure I could answer for Mr Grant when I said that we would be much obliged to him, and ready to serve him howsoever we could in heartfelt thanks for his pains.

I returned to Mr Grant with this good news and he was as surprised as

I was by the generosity of Mr Neve's offer. Here we had been expecting, from the tone of his book, that the gentleman would castigate us for our venality and lack of respect for the dead and that the best which we could hope for might be that he would accept our deep contrition now, indicated by my return of the hair, and he would quietly forgive us and not publish any further pamphlets about the affair. But instead he was not only forgiving us but also offering to help us, to assist me in reading and raising us up in society by inviting me to visit each week. It was hard to believe at first and Mr Grant sat quietly shaking his head at the strange turn of events.

'It is most unexpected, Mr G.' (We had resumed calling each other by our customary names, which in itself filled me with gladness since the formality of the last few weeks had had such a chilling effect on my spirits.) 'But if you were to meet the gentleman, I think you might more easily comprehend his offer. He is kindness and liberality itself. Maybe it is his years of reading and scholarship that have opened his heart and his judgement. After all, you yourself have always commended the wisdom which is to be found in books and particularly in the words of poets. I think perhaps the years that Mr Neve has spent immersed in the work of Milton and other writers have meant that he has learned compassion and a free and open mind about people.'

'You are probably correct, Lizzie,' said my husband. 'I had hoped to be able to interest you in the work of the poets myself. But sometimes those people who love us most do not make the best teachers. Maybe you will progress better in learning to read under the guidance of this great scholar and gentleman. This is indeed a very valuable opportunity for both of us, and you must certainly accept his kind proposal.'

I did not think it worth replying that I had already accepted Mr Neve's offer. It was enough for me that I now also had Mr Grant's blessing on the arrangement and that we were united in our decision to proceed in this manner. At one point, a few weeks previously, when Mr Grant had walked the streets alone each evening, it had seemed that we were in Hell and that it was in that infernal region that we would remain. With this new arrangement, there seemed to be some redemption, a solution that would allow my husband and me to grow closer together once more.

Now therefore I rise early every Friday, and walk quick as I can down across Cheapside to the river where all the stalls and barrels are drawn up as crowded as cockles at low tide, and I ignore all the rough sellers hawking their cheap oysters and eels and crabs, for nothing but the best mackerel will do for Mr Neve, and I buy it thinking of Satan and Moloch and all the other characters he has told me of, and then I hasten up the hill and through the streets, which gradually widen and grow more tranquil as I draw nearer to Holborn. The reading lesson begins as soon as I have drunk a cup of tea, and I have now grown so agile and accomplished a student that I can read the first two hundred lines of *Paradise Lost* slowly without assistance, and I thrill to the opening speech of Satan and his heroic defiance and scorn of the tyranny of Heaven, although Mr Neve tells me that Milton is showing us that the devil only uses clever rhetoric and is really deceitful, so I try dutifully to temper my admiration.

Then I busy myself in the kitchen preparing the dinner, baking the fish and steaming the vegetables – Mr Neve is very partial to green vegetables, more than anyone I have encountered before, and will swallow a cabbage faster than a good steak pudding any afternoon – and I set everything before him at the table just as he likes it. There is a decanter of wine too on the table, and many a bottle of port when he is entertaining company. For on frequent occasions, other literary and scholarly gentlemen join us for loud and lengthy dinners, or 'immortal dinners' as he calls them. Mr Hayley, another Milton scholar, is often in attendance and the sharp Mr Hazlitt and also Mr Lamb who has a merry wit and who will drink two whole bottles of wine all to himself. Those two are always talking about theatre and Shakespeare and the critics, so far as I can understand, for the conversation moves faster

and finer than a boxing cudgel, and I must pour the port and bring
in the next course, so I only catch snippets of the jokes and sallies as I
run in and out. And sometimes Mr Fuseli the artist joins them, a small
foreign man who never stays still and who strikes with barbs I cannot
follow, and a young surgeon called Mr Batty, who is full of passion about
poetry and old things. All these men are intrigued by my presence and
catch me round the waist as I approach the table and quiz me about
my knowledge of Milton and my life in Cripplegate and my opinion
on many matters. I try to give as good an account of myself as I can,
and they seem very pleased with what they hear, because they smile
and laugh and pinch me, and last week Mr Hayley even shouted out,
'Great God, Neve, where did you find this adorable creature?' and they
sometimes vie with one another as to who should invite me on his
knee and interrogate me on my latest lesson and my notions of Milton.

My life has changed utterly since the disinterment of the poet
some seven months ago. Indeed, I am not certain that my marriage
with Mr Grant will ever be the same as once it was. He has broken his
silence, and thus, now when we eat those pears I pickled last October,
we do, in truth, converse together, contrary to my former fears about
the continuing enmity between us. We discuss my progress with Mr
Neve, and my opinions of Milton, and he tries to encourage me to
broaden my reading and to study the newspaper too and learn about
the events in France and the growing ferment among the liberal groups
in London, but I am reluctant, for my mind is devoted only to Milton
and to *Paradise Lost*, and I do not care to exert myself for any other
cause. At this, sometimes, he grows a little pensive, and I wonder, on
certain days, whether he did not prefer me when I could not read a
word and I was content to learn only from him and to concern myself
with the house and the accounts and Mrs Hoppey and the business of
the parish. He is always particularly silent on Friday mornings, when
I have not the time to heat his porridge as usual, for I have to hasten
to Billingsgate, in order to find the best bargains of the day, but when,

on occasion, I have asked him about his concerns, he brightens and says, "'tis no matter", and that he is so much obliged to Mr Neve for excusing our transgressions and elevating our horizons. He feels the debt of gratitude that we owe Mr Neve most acutely, and never fails to pour out his praise whenever his name is mentioned.

As for myself, although it was with a degree of hesitation that I first ventured to Mr Neve's rooms in Holborn and chose to tell him the story of that fateful day in August, nevertheless truth, naked truth, I discovered, is a virtue, and there is a certain sweetness of relief in being able to give an account of what took place those few hot days in summer, which changed my life forever. How many nights had I lain awake, tossed by the fluctuations of anxious care and guilty pleasure! How often had I feared that the cold hand of Milton would grasp me as well as Mr Laming! But finding in Mr Neve a forgiving and wise listener, I have learned to forego any easy pleasures or excuses and to set out on a course of restraint and probity. Moreover, being persuaded that perhaps the reader may profitably learn from my narrative and forego all temptation and avarice in the future, I was justly eager to divulge my fatal secret, which has lived locked in the guilty bosom of my heart for far too long. Cold, indeed, will be the sensibility that will not tremble at my tale and shudder at the profanity of our deeds! Wise is he who heeds my warning and keeps the dead safe from all danger of violating hands! Now I know, from reading myself the devious persuasions of Satan, and the prudent guidance of Milton's God and the angel Michael, that I shall henceforth walk along the narrow road of righteousness, avoiding the errors and deviances of our first forebears. With Mr Neve as my guide, I take my first wandering and slow steps, certain that others will later follow in my path.

***

Postscript to the Reader

The author of the preceding memoir approached me in her hour of greatest need and threw herself upon my protection. Her angelic face and modest demeanour bespoke a life confined within the path of strictest virtue and belied the disreputable nature of her character and the iniquity of her recent deeds which she speedily disclosed to me and which clearly weighed heavily on her heart. Hers, it seemed, was a life now fallen upon ill times to be sure, but one which could only awaken the strongest pangs of pity in the heart of any sensitive observer. Nay, it could be argued that she was an innocent child, neglected by her feeble husband and led astray by the tough vulgar crowd among whom she had struggled to sustain an existence, like a wild flower pushing up amid the stony highway. No man with any degree of delicate sensibility or moral understanding would be able to withstand such an appeal to the tender possibility of his mercy, and I gladly offered what little succour I could give.

The events in Cripplegate in the summer of 1790 were well known to me. Indeed, I reported on the incident twice and was chiefly responsible for making publick this scandalous and sacrilegious action. But the involvement of women, and of Mrs Grant in particular, in these terrible deeds was as yet unknown to me, and caused me considerable unease. How could one so tender and amenable to all the calls of modesty and virtue be persuaded to act without any shame or recourse to the pangs of conscience or repentance? The wickedness and debauchery of her life was perhaps to be expected from one left so isolated in her youth and compelled to make the journey from country to city that has proved the familiar downfall of many untutored women in the past. But the complete absence of moral sense during the disinterment came as a shock to me and has troubled me greatly in the days since first I heard this tale.

Conversation and regular intercourse with those endowed with the finest sensibilities, however, have softened the brutal habits of this creature and rendered her mind capable of hearing the wise sentiments of the poet she once helped to destroy. Never have the immortal words of Milton been applied to better effect! Never has the act of reading his sublime verses produced a more immediate result, the restoration and improvement of one lost soul! I watch each week the poet's energy and intrepidity of mind strengthen her resolution to live a chaste life. I witness the influence of his integrity upon her young intelligence and I rejoice that I share with Milton the joy of bringing her to penitence and lawful behaviour.

There is, in Mrs Grant's tale, much which may be of advantage to the reader. Although the more vicious readers may take undue pleasure in the account of the disinterment and the cutting of the body, and in the later mercenary selling of the reliques, nevertheless the description of the sorrow and unhappiness of the parties, and the destruction of everything tender and lovely between them following the deed, should give every reader cause for reflection and push him to embrace restraint and respect for the dead, whenever his inclination may urge otherwise. The use of this story, in other words, pressed my hasty publication of a narrative that might otherwise have been better buried peacefully with the body it so violently awakened. This is the purpose for bringing so shameful and grotesque a deed to the attention of the publick once again, that the experience of Mrs Grant, beset on all sides by heavy guilt and yet not so far distracted that she was insensible to the divine injunctions of the Bard, may serve as a valuable lesson to those readers uncertain about the proper objects of respect in these tumultuous times.

Mrs Grant is supposed to be the author of her own history but, as she confessed to me freely, she cannot write and would be hard put to it to pen the narrative here placed before you. As far as I was able, I have recorded her words faithfully, but here and there it has been necessary to alter the stile and omit some of the more base details, particularly as far as the corpse and the grave are concerned, so as to give the story a more pleasurable and moral cast for the reader. Parts of the tale as told to me during our reading lessons were perhaps more suitable for the gutters of Fore Street than the withdrawing-rooms of Holborn or Mayfair. But the whole, drest in the simple garments of truth which requires no artificial adornment, will charm the most reluctant of readers and endear everyone to the original vibrant spirit of Elizabeth Grant.

Philip Neve, 8 February 1791

* * * * * * * *

My words and nobody elsses.

Misster neev as wrote all abowt my lyfe and givn mee a copie ov is paipers beeforr thaiy is turnd inta a book but i av not tol im evryfing becos i still as the bone from mister fownten wich i keep iden from evrywon I did not even tell mister grant but its still in my pettycoots and i will ide this wivit becos i dont want anywon to no that evry fryday wen i gos to misster neev i dont reely lern to reed much but i sits doyn wiv the book of Milton and mister neev sits beside mee but after i starts to say the words ee puts is arme abow my sholders and then ee reeches is and doyn into my boosom and ee tuches my brests and I keeps trying to say them words but then ee kisses the bak of my nek and i can feel is ot breff on mee sholders and rite doyn mee spyne but still i keeps trying to say them words wich are difecolt lik botomles perdishun and imortal wo and such but now ee plises the ova and under my dress and feels insyd my pettycoot and i moov a litl to put im off but ee is ryt strong and wont be put off and ee tuches mee and tikels mee and then i cant reed any longer for my mind is sumwer els doyn lower and

ee piks mee up and carees mee to is cowch and unbutons and ee tayks
mee ees much ruffer than meester grant and mister fownten sometimes
ee turns mee over and pushes is fing rite up mee ars and sometimes
ee goes in my mowth and other times ee jus tayks mee in the ushal
waiy but ee thusts reel hard an fast and i crie out wich ee reely lyks ee
tells mee it maikes im spowt morr ee ses so i dont lyk meeself becos
sometimes i lyk wot mister neev dos and i ackchully finks abowt it
kwite a lot all week but i nows its rong and so evry fryday i dont wont
to go to im but I must it is nessry to redeem myself and mister grant
thinks that i must to lern reeding and vertu if only ee new wot we did
but mister neev says i must tel nowon and if i tel then ee wil tel mister
grant abow mee and mister fowten doing it in the yard and then mister
grant will thro me out the owse onto the streets and also ee wil tel the
watchmen or the runners abow mister fownten and mister taylor and
the radicals and then ee will go to newgate becos of me wich i wood ayt
to appen so i keeps kwiet and i ait it but i go evry fryday and i maykes
mister neev appy and mister grant is as appy as ee will ever be now, tho
ee always loks sad sins we dug up milton and I wish we ad never foun
that wreched poet oo i detest and oo as roowind our lives and i wish
that i did not av to go to mister neev ever agen and i wish that i wos a
yong bryd agen and evryfing wos stil possibal becos i wos so luky but
i did not no it then but the only thing Ims glad abow now is that i av
my bon and it is mine and nobody nos abowt it and its my secret and
mine mine mine and i will never giv it to anywon i no that mister neev
as given away the hare that wos mister grants that i gav im ee gav it to
mister lam and mister batty as a present thay wos very pleesd becos they
lyke milton too so ee as not berried it agen like he sed ee wood that
wos a lie i suspect ees kept them bons as well ee is not as good as ee
says but I will never giv im my bon becos it is my secret and my liberty
I av neva wroot so much beforr but these are my words and nobody
elsses and I will ide this paper wiv the bon too so won day somewon wil
no the reel trooth of my story.

E.Grant. Cripelgate March 1791

THE END

Acknowledgements

This novel has gone through more transformations and "fine revolutions" than Milton's body and many people have read drafts and helped to shape its form. I am particularly indebted to the late Paul Marsh, to Bill Hamilton, and to Mark Brady, Sonia Devons and Chris Keil for casting their professional eyes upon it and helping to bring it to the light.

A number of friends have offered advice and encouragement during the process of disinterment, including Elizabeth Block, Lesley Downer, Peter Howarth, Sophie Jackson, Mari Jones, Fani Papageorgiou, Alastair Sim, Ali Smith, Maja Petrović-Šteger, Aleš Šteger. And of course my family has played a keenly supportive role throughout the excavation and production. Thanks to them all, and especially to Fleming, Gillian, George and Robert.

CillianPress|

www.cillianpress.co.uk

Lightning Source UK Ltd.
Milton Keynes UK
UKOW02f0844021215

263881UK00004B/111/P